JCP

D0906054

THE GIFT
OF THE MESTIZO

THE GIFT
OF THE
MESTIZO

•

Marjorie M. McGinley

AVALON BOOKS
NEW YORK

PRINTED IN THE UNITED STATES OF AMERICA
ON ACID-FREE PAPER
BY HADDON CRAFTSMEN, BLOOMSBURG, PENNSYLVANIA

To Douglas and Sharon

Chapter One

All he had to say was, everybody better stay out of his way! The anger was so built up inside that he was about to explode.

Ben Mitchell strode quickly out of the courtroom and across the street, then swung up on his yellowish-brown horse, Paddy. He backed the horse up a few steps, away from the hitching rail. Using the reins to turn the horse north, he rode up the street to the end of the dusty town of Websterville and out away from everyone.

He continued into the large, vacant dirt area, covered by sparse grass and an occasional prickly pear, surrounding the small one-street town.

He'd never come so close to violence in his life. He, who'd always been a nonviolent man.

That was why it was better that he just ride away, right now!

1

The rhythmical pounding of his horse's hooves was comforting as he rode away from town, putting distance between himself and those who had done him wrong.

Outright lies! Saying *he* was lying! And about things that *they* had done!

If he never saw any of them again, it would be too soon. He ached to have the comforting, smooth wooden handle of his Navy Colt in his hand and settle this problem right here and now. Walk back into that courtroom and—

No! Stop! Don't even think about that—but still . . . fancy legal paperwork, and he was out of his ranchland, and his ex-sister-in-law and her crooked new husband owned it!

And he knew his father back in Texas, if he was still alive, would probably have thought that the whole thing was all Ben's own fault for his carelessness.

He was sorely tempted to run back into that dangblasted courtroom and do a little corrective shooting to make things right and fair and *just!*

But if there was one thing both his parents had taught him it was that two wrongs don't make a right.

Violence wasn't the answer.

But that left one big question: Dang it, then, *what is the answer?*

What do you do when you are innocent and have been lied about and stolen from?

The horse's hooves carried him steadily and rhythmically away from the small town of Websterville, Arizona.

Why and how had it come to this? He began to think, to try and figure it out as he rode.

Perhaps what was wrong in the first place was going into partnership with his older brother Oliver after their parents had died. He and Ollie had left Texas five years ago and come to Arizona with enough money from the sale of the small Texas cattle ranch to buy land here, which they owned jointly.

Ollie was a good man and they had gotten along just fine; that is until Ollie married and brought Lucy to their small but prospering horse ranch on Cedar Creek.

That was a year ago.

From the very first he saw that Lucy wanted Ollie all to herself and wanted him—Ben—off the ranch.

Trouble was, he—Ben—owned half, and Ollie had asked him to stay, at least for a couple of years.

After both parents died, Ben and Ollie had decided that they wanted to raise horses rather than cattle.

They were trying to breed a slightly larger horse than the usual "cow pony", which tended to be on the small side, while still keeping all the good qualities of the breed. The cow pony was able to stop and turn quickly, was surefooted, courageous, and rugged. Cow ponies were also able to survive and thrive on the limited forage and water available here in the southwest.

Oliver was the one who handled the business end and Ben took care of the everyday workings on the ranch. Oliver was not a good horseman and needed Ben's wrangling skills as well as Ben's skill planning which horses to breed to produce the desired results.

And so Ben had reluctantly agreed, even though there was no love lost between himself and Oliver's new bride.

And then, three months ago, Ollie had been thrown from his favorite dun horse when he was out riding alone, and he had been dragged. His left foot had somehow gotten trapped in his stirrup.

He was dead by the time the horse returned home, still dragging Ollie.

Shortly after Ollie's funeral—too soon, in fact, to be seemly—Lucy began seeing David Woolsey, who conveniently worked in the Land Office. He was the Land Agent.

Lucy and David were married two months to the day after Ollie's death.

It had been a bitter day for Ben, to see his brother's petite widow laughing, smiling, and happy hanging onto the elbow of David's large arm in his new store-bought black suit.

Ben hadn't been invited to the wedding two weeks ago, but he'd been in town that day to buy a new rope. He saw the creamy-skinned, redheaded new bride in her white wedding dress. She was coming out of the little white church at the south end of town with her new husband, David.

As Ben went about his business in Cavanaugh's General Store, he heard the women gossips in town talking. They had stopped talking when they saw it was him, but he'd heard enough to know what they were saying. "Everyone knows," he'd heard Mrs. Goodrich say, "that the *second* time you are married, you don't wear white. How bold and brazen a woman is this Lucy person, anyway?"

How many times had he heard his own mother say that when he was a kid growing up? Even he, who knew next to nothing about the fine points of women's social rules and regulations, knew that.

It just wasn't done. And only two months after her first husband's death.

But what did Lucy care what anyone in Arizona Territory—in Websterville—thought?

Lucy Woolsey now. No longer Lucy Mitchell, Ollie Mitchell's wife.

She only came up to the middle of her second husband David's chest, Ben had noticed.

Ben had been standing on the sidewalk in front of Cavanaugh's General Store that day as she walked with her new husband from the church at the south end of the one main street to David's parents' house for the wedding reception. The senior Woolseys's house was out beyond the church. He saw Lucy and David's backs, mostly, as they walked away.

David was a big man. He wore his bushy yellow hair down to his shoulders in the fashion of men who were making the statement that they were not afraid of Indians. To wear your hair long was to say that you weren't afraid of being scalped. David was tall, slender, and heavily muscled. For some reason, perhaps the sun's effect on his light skin and hair, his face was always bright red. Unlike most men here, David did not usually wear a hat. From what Ben had heard about David, it seemed that he tended to be a pompous fool at times.

He and Ollie were both about five feet eight or nine. Or at least Ollie had been. . . .

David was five or six inches taller.

It was not long after the wedding—the day after, in fact—that Lucy presented Ben with paperwork which seemed to indicate that she and her new husband, David, owned the ranch and Ben was out.

Ollie had always taken care of all the ranch paperwork.

Conveniently—and stupidly on his part—Ben had left all the papers regarding the ranch in Ollie's "office" after Ollie's death. He knew now that that was a big mistake. That was what he knew his father would have disapproved of.

What he and Ollie had both called "the office" was just a big, crude pine desk in one corner of Ollie and Lucy's bedroom; by then the new widow's bedroom.

It hadn't seemed proper to go in there.

The new paperwork seemed to show that Ollie had bought Ben out two weeks before his death. The witnesses, supposedly, to the signing of the document were—conveniently—David Woolsey and his father, John Woolsey.

Lies, all lies.

The forgeries were excellent, even Ben had to admit that. His own signature was perfect. He wondered who had done it so well.

The day that Lucy had presented him with the forgeries, Ben had rushed into town to see his lawyer, Ephram Brazer.

Ephram was a tall, thin man with a long narrow face, who always looked vaguely worried. Always, before this, he'd done right by Ben and Ollie Mitchell.

Ephram had suggested that Ben move into one of the five rooms in the small hotel in town until the thing was settled. So Ben had been staying at Mercer's Hotel.

It was handy because it was right across the street from the courthouse.

It was just as well, because by that time Ben was tempted to ride right back out there to the ranch and beat the living daylights out of that *liar,* David Woolsey. David had been out there at the ranch standing side by side with Lucy when she presented him with the forged papers—for protection, probably. Protecting the poor defenseless widow, no doubt.

Even after thirteen long days in town, he had still wanted to punch that liar David, but Ephram said that that was the worst thing he could do.

So Ben had waited impatiently for the lawyers to do their work; sure that *somehow,* if he just kept telling the *truth,* everything would work out all right.

He had no problem with Lucy owning her half, as she was entitled to, being Ollie's widow. But, obviously, she had not been content with that.

Earlier this morning, when Ben was at a pre-court meeting at his lawyer's office in town, Ephram said that what it boiled down to in the end, was his word against Lucy's, David's, and David's father, John.

Three against one.

And David's father was the banker in town now. In church every Sunday, regular as clockwork. A deacon no less.

And as far as Ben himself knew, John Woolsey *was* a decent man.

Why? Why had John Woolsey lied?

Ben thought he knew the answer: Lucy. Lucy had some mysterious power over men. She had only to speak and men believed her.

So there it stood: Mr. Woolsey had lied and David and Lucy had the ranch and Ben had nothing but egg on his face.

Ephram said Ben was lucky he still had his horse. And the forgeries had stood as written; passed as the truth. Judge Colby had said so. At three o'clock, today. In the small, plain, plank-walled room off Sheriff Squibb's office that served as the local courtroom.

All the involved parties were sitting in front of the judge, who sat at a table in the back of the room.

His own lawyer, Ephram Brazer, had been no help. Ephram had agreed that the signatures were there, in black and white. There was nothing he could do.

"Well, where is the money I was supposed to have gotten from the sale?" Ben had demanded at one point in the proceedings.

"Probably safely in a bank in another town," Lucy's lawyer Roy Brady had said to the judge, not even getting up out of his chair to speak, with a look on his face that indicated that the lawyer thought that Ben was as low and despicable a human being as could be imagined.

Ephram looked at Ben with sympathy, but then shrugged his shoulders as if to say to Ben, "My hands are tied."

Ben had stared hard at John Woolsey in the courtroom, trying to will him to tell the truth. John wouldn't look him in the eye.

And what was worse, Lucy's lawyer insinuated that Ben was being seen in town as a liar, trying to take advantage of a poor little widow.

A poor little widow? Lucy was as helpless as a *scorpion or a rattler.*

Well, the town would get what they deserved. In time, they would learn what Lucy was really like. He'd seen her lie to Ollie about little things; like where she'd been. Ben had seen her someplace else from where she told Ollie she was, many times. She'd lied about things that seemed unnecessary to lie about— like saying she was at the general store when she was at the hat shop.

Why lie about nonsense like that? Ollie didn't deserve that. Ollie didn't care whether she was at the grocer's or the milliner's when she went to town. But Lucy just seemed to *want* to lie about everything; like she found it exciting to lie and not get caught. Ben really didn't understand it.

He watched Paddy's head and mane bobbing in from of him as he rode north, thinking. He was resisting the urge to change directions and ride east to Texas where he was born. But there was no family left there. His mother and father were dead. His father had died of a heart ailment and his mother had died of fever two months later.

They knew he had never been a liar. They knew his word was his bond. The whole thing was preposterous.

Ben had been so confident that the truth would come out that he'd checked himself out of Mercer's Hotel and packed up his things on his gelding; sure that at the very least, they would offer to buy out his share of the ranch. David was known to have plenty of money.

But today, Judge Colby had chosen to believe Lucy, David, and John Woolsey. The three Woolseys. It was done, and there was nothing legally, Ephram said, that Ben could do about it.

There was no sense running away back to Texas. There was nothing for him there now, except a few families—neighbors—that he had grown up with. There was no way anyone back in Texas could help him, anyway.

He came to the top of a rise and stopped to let Paddy rest. He was so angry, he *still* wanted to turn back and blow a few lying, crooked heads off. Not Lucy's of course; he would never hurt a woman, no matter how evil, crooked, and wrongheaded she was. But he wouldn't mind blasting a few holes in David, the land thief, and David's rotten, lying father, John.

He didn't blame his own lawyer, Ephram, or David's lawyer, Roy Brady. He doubted that they were in on it. They had both expressed honest surprise when they had first heard—from Lucy—that Ben had sold out to Ollie like that.

But they believed that he did.

It would have been logical, Roy Brady said, given that Ollie was a married man and all, and that Ollie would want the ranch for himself and his new bride. Ben suspected that Ephram secretly agreed.

But they were stupid too. If he'd sold out to Ollie, wouldn't Ollie have come into town right away and registered the change?

He'd said that to them today.

"Probably just hadn't gotten around to it," Lucy's lawyer Roy said. "Ever'body knows how busy a rancher is. Takes time to get around to things like that. Probably didn't think there was any need to hurry."

That part was logical. Everyone in that courtroom knew that Ollie didn't know he would be dead so soon.

Chapter Two

J udge Colby, a large fat man with drooping brown hooded eyes and large jowls, had very faintly bobbed his head in agreement. When Ben saw that, he knew he had lost.

Dang it!

He had sensed a mean streak in Lucy from the very first time he saw her. Why hadn't Ollie seen it? *Ollie, how could you be so blind?*

Her dark red curly hair, smooth skin, and deep blue eyes had put the fever into Ollie from the first day he saw her getting off the stage.

Ollie had come home raving about the small woman with the red hair and a blue dress. "She has such a tiny waist, I bet I could put my hands right around it," Ollie had said, dancing around the front porch of the ranch house in happiness. "She came right up and talked to me," Ollie had said in amazement. "Asked

12

me the way to the hotel! Don't know how she didn't see it for herself—it was right there in front of her. But I showed her. Yes, indeedy, I showed her. Even carried her bags inside for her. She's a little tiny thing, Ben," Ollie had said. "Cute as a button. Has a couple of the cutest dimples in her cheeks!"

It was not long after that that Ben had met Lucy. Ollie brought her to the ranch to show her off proudly to Ben.

Ben had thought she was all right, at first, until one day he caught her slapping Miguel, the old Mexican man that had been their cook for many years. He had come with them from Texas, where he had worked for Ben and Ollie's parents practically all his adult life.

He was over seventy, and Ben thought that he was a good sport to pick up and move with Ollie and Ben to a new place when he was so old. Ben thought a lot of the old man.

But Miguel apparently did things too slow for Lucy's taste. Ben walked into the kitchen one day when Lucy was out visiting at the ranch, and he caught her slapping the old man in the face.

"Hurry up, you old fool," she had said, as she hit the dignified old man. "You think we can wait forever for that coffee?"

The old man felt shamed, Ben knew. His pride was hurt. He was a proud man; he didn't deserve that kind of treatment. Lucy had no business hitting Miguel or anyone!

He couldn't help it; his temper had flared. What

right did she have to hit Miguel? Who did she think she was?

"Don't you ever hit Miguel again!" Ben had roared, louder than he had meant to. After he yelled, his teeth gritted in anger at her arrogance that she thought she was allowed to hit Miguel because he was hired help. Besides, whether he was paid or not, Miguel was family to Ben.

She was neither intimidated nor frightened.

Miguel hurried out of the room.

"Don't you *ever* tell me what to do!" she said.

She left the room in a huff and went and found Ollie and told Ollie that Ben had been mean to her for no apparent reason.

Ben had soon learned that it was useless talking against Lucy to Ollie. He turned a deaf ear. He always took Lucy's side. Believed everything she said.

A week later, Miguel had quietly left, going back to Texas. Now Ben understood that the old man was smart; he had seen what was coming.

The trouble started the day Lucy had come up to Websterville from Tucson. He and Ollie's lives had gone downhill after that.

Not that he blamed her for Ollie's death; only for the way that she had driven a wedge between Ollie and himself. Before that, Ben and Ollie had always been close, but poor Ollie was now caught in the middle between the two of them.

She had wanted to be the boss, not only of Ollie, but of Ben and the whole ranch. More than once, even after she and Ollie were married, she and Ben had clashed, even though he had purposely tried to keep his distance.

He remembered that one day she came out of the door and onto the ranch-house porch as he was riding by, and called him over.

"Hitch up the wagon and drive me into town," she said. "I want to do some shopping."

He was already mounted, on his way to round up some ten or twenty stray horses. The strays had wandered and were heading into an area of damp meadow near the creek. Locoweed had begun to grow there. He told her that, as politely as he could. In truth, he also wanted to check and see if any of the steers they kept on the ranch for eating had wandered there also.

"I don't care about a couple of horses going crazy. I want to go to town," Lucy had said, crossing her arms and angrily stamping her foot as she stood on the ranch-house porch. He knew by now that she was used to getting her own way and didn't like it when she was crossed. She was acting like a spoiled brat.

"You can boss Ollie all you want, but not me," Ben had said gently to her. "You don't own me, or my half of this ranch."

Well, he said bitterly to himself, *I guess she took care of that little problem.*

Not for the first time, Ben wondered if she had just married Ollie for the ranch. She sure hadn't seemed devoted to Ollie at all. He had sensed a vague disappointment in Ollie since the wedding.

Now there was no doubt that she was crooked as well. He suspected the forgeries were her work. She must have spent hours perfecting writing his and Ollie's signatures after Ollie's death.

And the truth was, how could he honestly blame Ollie for not seeing through her when he, himself, had never given thought—never for a moment thought it *necessary* to run into his dead brother's bedroom to get ahold of the papers showing ownership of the ranch? It had barely crossed his mind to go in Ollie's bedroom and go through the desk and do anything about the ranch's ownership papers, before he dismissed the idea as improper.

The *real* papers.

What a fool! What a dang fool! How could he have been so stupid? And not just a moment ago blaming Ollie for not knowing what Lucy was like? *And I was just as stupid?*

By now he understood her well enough to know that Lucy would not be dumb enough to leave the real joint ownership papers anywhere where he could go and search and find them.

She had probably destroyed them.

If not, she certainly wouldn't leave them in Ollie's desk where Ben could go and get them back. She might be many things, but she was far from being a fool. A trip to the ranch would be useless, and the law against him on that, especially now. Probably give David Woolsey or a hired gun a chance to shoot him, saying Ben came to kill them or something.

No, he'd never give them a chance to hurt him again.

He rode north instead, toward the canyon area. An area where nobody could find him.

Alone, that's what he wanted to be; alone so that people couldn't find him! He wanted to get away from people.

People cause you so much dang-blasted trouble in your life! And none of it your own doing!

Greed. That's what caused it. That's what it was all about: greed. Lucy and David's and yes, maybe even David's father's greed.

He had figured out where he would go. He would head to what some people called the Lost Prospector Canyon area.

It was an area most people avoided.

A prospector named Samuel Logan had gone into one particularly mazelike canyon in that area ten years ago, in 1868, never to be seen or heard from again. Sam Logan's two mules—one pack mule and one mule he rode—showed up months later back in Websterville, with no sign of Sam Logan. The two mules were gaunt and skinny, as if they had gone through a terrible ordeal.

Some of the canyons where Ben was going were so big and deep that no one would find him, either, if anything happened to him in one of them. But the good news was that most of the canyons had creeks or streams in the bottoms of them, and game was abundant.

Some of the canyons where he was headed were so inaccessible that they had never had a human being in them yet, some people said; and some said that maybe there never would be.

Even Indians wouldn't bother to go there. At least, not now. There were signs in some of the canyon bottoms and canyon tops that centuries ago, people lived there.

A few years ago, when he had explored the very beginning of the canyon area with Ollie, he remembered they had discovered squatty rock buildings on one of tablelands above the canyons. He saw that a lot of thought went into the construction. The rooms were all attached so as to get the wisest use of rock walls. Get the side walls for two rooms out of building one wall. Keep out the winter cold better too. He had a lot of admiration for the long-ago builders.

The last time he had been there, the walls of the crumbling buildings were only as high as his shoulders. He had always wondered if he would have been able to stand straight up inside when they were first built.

The ceilings—long gone now with the walls just standing there open to the sky—probably were not much over five feet high when they were new, so he guessed that the people living there were short. But that was only a guess on his part. He had no real way of knowing.

Although he knew why the people had built on the canyon top—probably for protection—he also knew that that meant lugging water up from the canyon bottom some parts of the year. And collecting rainwater other parts of the year. It was a problem that he would have to face if he chose to live on a canyon top.

He'd brought with him a tin bucket for that purpose, that he'd bought in the general store in Websterville a few days ago. Buying the tin bucket was the one admission to himself that he had some idea of the outcome of the court case.

The bucket was inside one of the two large canvas bags hanging from his saddle. Some onions and potatoes were packed inside the bucket. The other canvas bag was filled with food items too. He also had a long rope coiled in front of him, hanging from his saddle, and his blanket. A slicker was rolled up inside his blanket.

Luckily, his horse, Paddy, was one of the larger horses he'd bred and didn't seem to mind the extra weight. He planned to eat the heaviest item, the potatoes, first. But not tonight. It was beginning to be too dark to see, and he'd have to stop for the night.

A few minutes later, as night drew on, he camped, taking care of Paddy first, before he pulled jerky and biscuits out of his saddlebags and ate a miserable, lonely, cold supper. He drank water from his canteen.

Only from exhaustion was he able to give up stewing and going over and over things in his mind, trying to think of what else he could have done back there in town. He rolled himself into his gray blanket in the darkness, used his saddle as a pillow, and slept.

At dawn, he was back up on his horse and heading northward, without taking time to eat. There was no trail, but he remembered the way from when he and Ollie. . . .

Bitterly, he shook his head and tried to make himself think of something else. Not about Ollie. Not about things that he and Ollie had done together. He felt so alone without his big brother with him in this world.

Ollie, how could you have done this to me?

The morning passed. A few times he stopped to rest his horse and a few times he walked alongside Paddy to give the short, sturdy, claybank a rest.

Paddy was a yellowish horse, the color of clay. Ben was proud of him. He had been one of the first bred at the ranch on Cedar Creek. His mother was a sorrel and his father was a dun—the usually quiet, dependable horse that Ollie had been riding that day . . . Ollie.

Stop it. Think about something else!

At least he had supplies. If things had worked out right, he had planned to take the supplies back to the ranch to use. If not. . . . He had oats for Paddy, coffee, the potatoes, beans, onions, bacon, ham, salt, and flour, among other things.

At noon, he stopped and fried some bacon and potatoes and onions, and made coffee. Then he set off again. The weather was just right. There wasn't a cloud, just clear blue sky, and the temperature was perfect.

He had on his usual clothing. He favored flannel or cotton solid color shirts and black trousers and boots. He liked black hats as well. Today he had on a dark brown cotton shirt.

Late in the afternoon, walking beside Paddy to give the horse a rest, he stopped for a moment to watch a mother deer and her fawn. The fawn must have been born this very spring. The two of them were about ten feet below him in a rocky, sloping area, nibbling the leaves off some bushes. They seemed unaware of him.

As usual, he was amazed that they grazed on such a steep slope so casually. They didn't seem at all worried about falling. He wondered if the mother deer ever worried about the fawn. If he was down there with a human child he'd be frightened to death that the child would fall. He sat, silent, watching them until they finished eating at that particular bush, and moved on.

Just before dusk, he stopped again and made camp. He took care of Paddy, made a small fire, and put coffee on to boil. There was plenty of firewood as there were no people using it up here on this empty, high plateau. He pulled out some ham and a couple of potatoes, sliced them into a frying pan, and put them on the fire. He added a sliced onion.

He'd been going upward all day. The land had been sloping up, sometimes gently, sometimes more steeply. Finally it had flattened out. But he had a sense of being high, up on this plateau, much higher than back down there in the Websterville area.

This was an area of limestone rock, mostly pale yellow, sometimes with gray or pink layers in it. There were no mines up here, as there were surrounding Websterville, especially in the past. In fact, Websterville had begun as a mining supply town, which was why there was a small courtroom on the one main street.

This kind of rock apparently didn't hold ore, or if it did, it was too far from anywhere to be bothered with. Too far to lug back to Websterville, which was the closest town.

With so much land available for prospecting, it was no wonder people chose to stay south. To stay below this area where to go a few short miles from here to there, you might have a day's ride down into a canyon and then another day's ride up the other side, just to go a short distance "as the crow flies".

If you even could.

Some of those canyons had no way up and down; just sheer steep cliffs on both sides, hundreds of feet high. And there was no way wagons could bring ore out from steep, deep canyons.

Prospecting was easier in the southern part of the territory than here in the canyon land—not that it was all that easy down there, either, because of the scarcity of water.

Worse, the trails that there were, up and down through the canyons, were made up of the type of soil that didn't show horse's hooves or footprints, and there was even less chance of seeing a moccasin print to find your way back out. They were like labyrinths or mazes—the wind might very easily blow your tracks away so that you couldn't find your way out.

A series of winding passages with high rock walls, some with sharp horseshoe turns, was what the bottom of a lot of the canyons looked like. And in some parts the river made it impassable. Blocked your way.

It would be easy to get lost, he thought. Then he realized that he didn't need to worry about it; you're not lost if you don't give a hoot where you are.

He remembered from the last time he had been in this area with Ollie that they had discovered that sometimes, you could recognize a path or trail only by the fact that no vegetation grew there.

Then you didn't know if it was an animal trail down to the water at the bottom of the canyon, or a trail that people—ancient or recent—had made.

But that was all right. He didn't want to see people, anyway.

All of you, just leave me alone! he thought angrily.

His food was ready, and he ate. He must have been hungry. He felt less foul-tempered after he ate.

He went to check on Paddy, and made sure the rope was secure and the picket well into the ground so that Paddy was secure for the night.

Tomorrow he'd be reaching the big, deeper canyon he had in mind. The Lost Prospector canyon. He'd have to make a decision as to which way to go; whether to find a way down, or whether to stay atop the tableland where he was.

Chapter Three

Early the next morning, he made coffee and ate the last of the biscuits he had brought. He had to dunk the biscuits into the coffee to soften them, for they had become hard as rocks.

That was all right.

He was a pretty good biscuit-maker if he did say so himself, and either later today or tomorrow he would drag the ingredients out of one of the cloth provision bags hanging from his saddle and make some new ones. Need to put some beans to soaking overnight, tonight too. Cooked a lot quicker when you did that.

At noon, he chewed on a bit of deer jerky as he rode.

He had to admit he missed the horses back at the ranch, especially the new foals, and even the small one-room foreman's house two hundred yards off to the side of the main ranch house, where he had moved when Ollie married Lucy. It seemed like such a long time ago. So much had happened since then.

He was glad that his mother had not lived to hear about Ollie's death.

Everyone always said, his mother made the best jerky around, but he was not a fan of either beef or deer jerky, to tell the truth. He preferred ham or bacon, but it came in handy, like now, when he didn't want to stop to cook.

He stopped near a small drainage area where a small trickle of water ran down a slope, and let Paddy drink and rest. He refilled the two large canteens which hung from his dark brown leather saddle before he remounted and left.

Although he was on what he still considered table-land, he was still gently going up. In lower areas, the edges of canyons were concealed by prickly pear, junipers, ocotillos, and scattered pin oaks. He had to be careful. Here, it was turning into an area of junipers and pinyon trees.

As he rode upward, the juniper and pinyon trees thinned out and he found himself in an area of mostly yellow pines, although he still came upon an occasional juniper or pinyon tree here and there. Late in the afternoon, as he traveled through the pines, he thought he heard the sound of wild turkeys off to the left. Something must have disturbed them for them to be gobbling so loud this time of the day. It might have been a small family squabble, as they quieted down quickly.

Just before nightfall he arrived at the crest of the

first great canyon on the high plateau. Well back from
the edge, he camped for the night. He started a small
fire and then made himself some coffee and new biscuits and fried some bacon with some potatoes.

When he was through eating, he cleaned out the pan
and put about five big handfuls of beans in water to
soak overnight.

He looked around, carefully. Besides the pines there
were clumps of bear grass and yuccas growing in the
cracks between the giant flat boulders that made up
the tableland next to the canyon. The yuccas and the
bear grass grew in the cracks because small amounts
of soil had collected there.

The next morning, he took care of Paddy, then picketed the horse and walked for a mile or two along the
edge of the canyon, looking for a trail to go down.

There was none. Down below him, on the slopes,
he could see occasional prickly pear cactuses growing,
and shrubs. It was amazing how they had the ability
to hang on and grow on such steep slopes.

For a few minutes, he watched a red-tailed hawk
flying down in the canyon below him. Its gliding ability with just the slightest move of a wing tip was a
thing of graceful beauty.

He walked back and packed up, rode a mile or two
further along the top of the canyon, and repeated the
same procedure. He dismounted and took a drink.
Paddy nuzzled him affectionately, trying to poke his
nose under Ben's arm.

Mounting up, he rode still further along the top of
the canyon.

Still no way to go down.

He thought to himself that he was lucky it was early June, when the weather was not yet unbearably hot down in the canyon bottoms. In fact, so far, it had been beautiful weather all the way, with bright blue clear skies most of the time, and white, fluffy late afternoon clouds, although it cooled down quickly at night.

In the far distance and to his left, it looked as if it were raining. Miles and miles away.

The sun was clear and bright here, where he was. There was no sign of rain. The rocks facing him across the canyon on the other side were a strange color: a grayish-pinkish-brown that was like no color he had ever seen. He didn't think this odd color even had a name.

The rain never came close to where he was riding. The thunderstorm, if that's what it was, stayed far in the distance. The birds he saw were, for the most part, ravens. Shiny, black ravens.

It was late afternoon when he saw what looked like a trail down into the canyon. There was a wide ledge. The solid, wide, safe-looking ledge made a sharp switchback bend to the right, and looked as if it went downward. He could see where the ledge continued on down, then switched and came back this way well below him.

He hesitated about what to do.

Would Paddy be able to go down this trail without getting frightened and bolting and falling off the ledge, dragging them both to their deaths?

Would the ledge disappear halfway down and leave him stranded with nowhere for Paddy to turn around?

The last time he and Ollie had been in these canyons was about—what was it?—two years ago. Ollie was a little over twenty-five, and he, Ben, had been twenty-four.

He and Ollie had been riding mules that they had brought from Texas: their father's dependable gray-brown mules, Sassy and Stumpy. Now Lucy owned Sassy and Stumpy.

Sassy had one thing wrong with her. She liked to chew saddle blankets. You always had to be on the lookout to keep the saddle blankets out of her reach.

Mules were good for traveling in canyon country. But horses? It would be taking a chance. Should he? How did he feel about his luck today?

He'd always secretly called himself Bad Luck Ben. The only kind of luck he ever had, was bad. That was why he never played cards for money. He'd learned that lesson the hard way. It was always Ollie who seemed to have all the luck. At least, before. Now even Ollie's luck had run out.

What should he do?

He wanted to explore the canyon bottom.

He thought some more, then decided that the best thing to do was to picket Paddy one more time and start down the trail and see if it was wide enough—safe enough—to take his horse down.

The trouble was, he knew from past experience that it was probably at least a three-hour trip down. So at the very least, he'd be gone six hours.

He decided that it would be best if he waited for morning, just after dawn, to begin. That way, he would be back not too long after noon.

This would be a good campsite, right near the trail down. Nearby, there was another water drainage ditch. It had been formed by rain runoff from a higher area of the canyon top. There was just enough running water in the drainage ditch so that he would be able to get water for himself and Paddy, and his cooking needs. He had no idea if the water was a permanent-type thing or if it would dry up.

His best guess was that in a few days, it might be gone. He had no way of knowing. He figured that it had rained hard, at least once up here, in the days before he arrived.

He spent the rest of the afternoon choosing a good spot to picket Paddy in the morning, far back from the canyon edge where there were tufts of bear grass for Paddy to graze on.

He used to have only a wooden stake and a rope to picket his horse, but a few years ago he'd bought a sturdy metal stake with a metal ring on it from the blacksmith in town. He used a soft cotton rope tied to it, to picket Paddy. Then he ate some of the biscuits he had made the night before, as well as some of the beans.

Later, he watched squirrels playing and hunting things to eat near the edge of the canyon. *Squirrels always seem to be nervous,* he thought to himself. He noticed that there were a lot of squirrels close to the edge of the canyon.

Toward dusk he walked again to the canyon rim, and he noticed that there were a lot of ravens here also. For some reason, they all gathered at the edge of the canyon, the same as the squirrels did.

He guessed the ravens looked down into the canyons to watch for available food. They also raised their young safely on the ledges below the rim, where most predators couldn't reach the baby birds.

The one other bird that he could see many of was some kind of bird that looked like a swift. They flew— often in small groups—below him as he watched from the edge of the canyon. The shape of their wings and the way they flew reminded him of bats.

He watched the red and purple sunset near the edge of the canyon, and then went back to his campsite. He rolled into his gray blanket and slept, as soon as it was dark. Nights got cold swiftly up here.

Just after dawn, as soon as it was light enough to see, he watered and fed Paddy, and picketed him, far back from the edge of the canyon. Then he walked back to his campsite, took one of the two large round filled canteens, and some ham and biscuits, and walked back to the ledge.

He started down.

He had walked downward for fifteen minutes before he realized that it was not going to be an easy walk. He was thirstier than he expected, and it seemed like gravity was pulling him down. It was tiring on his leg muscles.

He saw a brown wren with a white chest land in a scrubby bush that jutted out of the dirt just below the ledge. The ledge was wider in spots than he had thought. When he was about a quarter of the way down he realized that it was a trail that had been used before. He thought that Paddy could safely make it down. There were even some places—out of sight from where he had been able to see from the top, where he thought that he could turn Paddy around if it became necessary.

By the end of the third hour, he was near enough to see the end—the canyon bottom—and the rest of the trail down. It was clear. There was no need to go further.

He could go back up, and tomorrow, he and Paddy would start again at dawn and go down.

He had to rest before he began the upward trip.

He sat down, put his back against the rock, and ate. He could see out over the ledge and down. The river in the bottom of the canyon looked red from here. He could have sworn that the last time he was here, the river was green. And there was evidence that there was plenty of game. He thought he could make out game trails through the brush at the bottom of the canyon.

In a few minutes, he stood up and began walking back upward. It was more tiring than he expected and his thirst was enormous. It seemed as if the very air sucked the moisture out of him. Even though he licked his lips, they were dry again rapidly.

He had to fight the urge to drink all the water before he got to the top. He knew that that would be stupid. He had to dole it out to himself bit by bit, he told himself.

Going up was worse than going down. He had to stop and rest every half hour or so. He was not sorry when he saw that last sharp switchback near the top come into sight.

Reaching the rim, he sat and rested a little way back from the canyon's edge for a few minutes before he went back to check on Paddy.

Paddy whinnied when he saw Ben come into sight. Unlike Ben, Paddy liked the company of people and other animals. He stroked Paddy and talked to him for a few minutes, then moved the picket rope to fresh grass.

Then he went back to his campsite. Nothing had disturbed it. That was good. He'd found no other place that looked as if it might be a better trail down into the canyon.

He ate and settled down for the night.

In the morning, he took care of Paddy and ate. After that, he saddled Paddy and packed everything up. He was careful to pack things so that they wouldn't do any rattling or moving about, and hung the carefully packed cloth bags off the saddle.

Still, he was worried.

He knew that there was no guarantee that any part of the ledge he had chosen wouldn't crumble and fall under the weight of him *and Paddy*.

Or would Paddy get frightened and rear up, or bolt, or fall and plunge them both over the side of the ledge?

He wasn't quite trembling, but he was worried and nervous as he led Paddy to the downward ledge.

Chapter Four

Slowly and cautiously he brought Paddy to where the yellow gelding would begin his first few steps downward on the ledge.

Leading Paddy by the halter, and talking softly to him, Ben began, a step at a time, to cautiously lead the gelding toward the ledge, and the downward canyon trail.

He stayed in front, going first, so that Paddy could see him as they began down the five-foot-wide ledge on the canyon rock wall. In some places the ledge was wider, but it never seemed less than five feet wide.

He didn't realize that he was holding his breath until a feeling in his chest told him of an urgent need for him to breathe.

Paddy's vision was limited mostly to the sides, and Ben watched the front. They made a good pair, he thought. They were depending on each other. On

Paddy's part, he was displaying a lot of trust in Ben. Ben felt a moment of great affection for Paddy. It only added to his sense of responsibility in this.

Ben realized that the horse, although nervous and staying near the inside of the ledge as much as possible, was game to follow him all the way down into the canyon. Paddy's eyes rolled a few times, but he didn't pull back or rear up, or worse, push Ben forward by crowding him.

It was a nerve-racking descent, nevertheless.

A few times, knowing the horse was as thirsty as he was, he stopped in a wider spot to pour water into his black hat and let Paddy drink.

It took over four hours to get down to the canyon bottom leading Paddy. When he was nearing the bottom, he breathed a big sigh of relief. The day he had first arrived at the canyon top and looked down, the water in the canyon bottom was a coppery-red color. Today, the water was back to green.

What a drastic change—a rich, dark green to a silty bright orange-red, and then back to green again.

A magic river.

He was relieved when he and Paddy reached the bottom.

Would Paddy be as eager, and willing to go up, if and when the time came that they needed to?

Upriver or down? Which way should they go?

He looked. The way downriver seemed easier. In some places the bottom of the canyon was wide; in other places it looked narrow. Here, at least, it was not so narrow that they couldn't travel along next to it.

He checked Paddy's horseshoes—they were fine.

He led Paddy for about fifteen minutes, but seeing that it was all right, he mounted up and rode. He was right; there were many game trails in and among the bushes.

What was he looking for?

He didn't know; he wasn't sure what he was looking for. Some place that said to him either *stay,* or some place to explore. He had no worries about food for at least a week or two. He had plenty for himself, and oats for Paddy. He had his pistol and his rifle for food, if necessary. And plenty of coffee. That was the most important thing. He didn't want to run out of coffee. Whatever else he ate or drank, he didn't care, as long as he had coffee.

He also liked drinking water. He hoped that the river might stay green for quite a while, as he didn't want to have to use his one extra blue shirt to filter the red silt out.

He looked around.

It was very different down here at the bottom of the canyon. A different world from up above.

A shrunken world, as you could only see short distances across and then look up, way up, steeply, on two sides in many places. The giant overall view from the top was gone. In its place—high, high walls on both sides. And a lot warmer, for June, than up on the plateau.

It had looked like bare rock from way up, but now that he was down here and close, he could see that scrubby brush and trees dotted the canyon bottom more than he realized.

He filled both canteens, luckily, because although he had seen no rain or rain clouds, and heard no thunder, he saw that the river had begun to turn red again and he knew that it had rained somewhere upstream. He found that the river rose rapidly after it rained upstream.

He was learning a lot, quickly.

He spent most of the day looking at the colors of the rocks in amazement. No plain gray canyon walls like back home near Websterville. Here they were that pinkish gray-brown light color.

He camped for the night in the mazelike canyon of rocks.

He fed Paddy oats. There was nothing much for Paddy to eat here, although Paddy tried chewing on some bushes.

When he camped for the night, he discovered that one of his brown socks had sprung a good-sized hole in the heel.

Dang, he said to himself. It was his only pair.

Around noon the next day, he dug around in the bottom of one of the saddlebags and found his razor and the small tin container which held a bar of soap. He took the soap and bathed in the river, washing his clothes at the same time. Then he shaved, using his hand to feel where he had missed, as he had no mirror.

He packed up and spent the rest of the day riding around, still heading west—downstream.

It was a day and a half later that he came upon

something odd. It was midafternoon. He was just about ready to sit under a tree and take a rest for a while when something about one of the canyon walls began to look strange to him.

He was in a wide-bottom canyon area, and the walls here were more yellow than what he had come upon so far. It was a yellow limestone or sandstone area, although above it, high up, there were the usual pinkish-gray layers.

But something more than the color attracted his attention. It looked liked—but it couldn't be—stairs. Faint traces—shapes—of stairs leading up the far left side of the canyon wall.

He would have to cross the river to get to it.

The river looked neither deep nor fast-moving here, as this was a place where both the canyon and the riverbed were wide. It was not one of those narrow places where the river was forced to speed up and rush and tumble through close, steep canyon walls.

The question was, should he ride across the river, or attempt to swim or wade?

The steps on the wall across the river disappeared out of sight as they went around a bend in the canyon to the right.

He decided to chance wading across, hoping that his supplies would end up drier if he led Paddy across rather than riding.

He picketed Paddy on this side of the river, away from a clump of stubby, barrel-shaped cactuses that seemed to be thriving down here, then waded across, holding his saddlebags and the two large cloth bags with his food items in them over his head. Because the river was so wide here, it was less than waist deep.

Leaving the saddlebags and the cloth bags on the other side, he came back over and led Paddy across. Tying Paddy to a short, scrubby pine tree on the other side, he put the saddlebags back on the horse and tied the food bags back on the saddle.

Removing his Navy Colt, he put the sixth bullet in. He usually rode with an empty cylinder, so the gun wouldn't go off accidentally. He clicked the cylinders shut and returned it to the holster, making sure his pistol was loose.

He left his Remington rifle in its sheath on Paddy. Any shooting he would need to do on the ledge and the "stairs" cut into the canyon wall, would be up close. The Colt was better.

He walked over to the stairs, marveling that anyone would have the patience and energy to carve stairs out of a canyon wall. Was it some ancient people who had done this?

From the way the edges were still sharp-looking— not worn away, as if they had been there for centuries—he guessed that someone had done this more recently.

How would they react to his intrusion . . . if anyone was still here?

With a shotgun blast?

Arrow through the heart? Was it Indians?

He decided that when he reached the part where he had to go around the bend in the canyon wall, he would go very, very slowly and carefully.

Who was it; who would be up here in this inaccessible area—besides himself?

He took his canteen and slung it over his shoulder, then walked over to where the stairs began. He backed up as close to the wall as he could and began to go up the stairs as quietly as possible. He had his pistol out and ready. One, two, three, four, five, six, seven, eight, nine stairs. He reached the ledge and slowly, slowly crept toward where the ledge went around a sharp bend in the rock wall.

He pushed his hat back and let it hang down his back by its strings as he peeked around the bend in the wall.

The ledge—which looked like a natural one, such as the one he had come down into the canyon on—led gently upward for twenty feet, then leveled out again as it came to another bend in the rock wall. So far, quiet and safe. Nothing there.

The second bend was five feet ahead. He could feel his heart pounding in his chest as he started to go around it, peeking ahead as he went.

He saw that there was a wide, natural overhang probably created centuries ago when the river was high enough and forceful enough to have dug out a ledge this high up, and there was a rock-walled house twenty feet away on a wider section underneath the overhang.

A strange looking white-haired man sat in the doorway on an old faded white, turquoise, and black woven, fringed Navaho rug. It was too late to withdraw; the old man had seen him.

He had on an old, faded light brown cloth shirt and light brown pants made of the same very old material. He had leathery brown skin which had spent many years in the sun and had become very wrinkled. His face must have been handsome once, as he had pleasant, even features.

"You can put that pistol 'way, 'less you're planning some killing," the man said, in an odd accent. There appeared to be no fear in what he said—he did not seem to be afraid of death. And the way he spoke . . . ? Ben couldn't decide whether it sounded like a Mexican accent or an Indian accent.

Ben put his pistol back in his holster, and his hat back on his head.

"What are you doing here?" Ben asked in surprise, walking along the ledge toward the man. "Are you alone here?"

Without smiling, but without meanness also, the old man said, "I could ask you the same. You are the first person—man, woman, or child—I have seen in a very long time."

He motioned for Ben to walk over closer and sit down.

Ben sat.

One question that Ben wanted to ask was how the man survived without a gun to shoot game. It was something he, himself, was worried about: how would he survive after he had used up all his ammunition?

Then he looked carefully and saw that he did not need to ask. The ancient-looking man was working on a snare. Two or three new snares of different types were already completed and lying next to the man on the colorful blanket. Sharp pointed sticks with loops and slip knots made of something—what was it?

He looked closer and saw.

Next to the man was a long length of cedar wood. The bark had been removed and the fibers under the bark had also been stripped.

The man was so experienced that as Ben watched him work on the long cedar fibers, he was reminded of his mother knitting. She had been able to knit seemingly without paying attention; she could talk and carry on a conversation while the knitting needles flew in her hands.

The old man's hands did the same. He folded the fibers not in half, but with one long strand and one short strand.

Then, after leaving a small loop, he began wrapping the long end around the shorter end, and as he talked he firmly spliced a new piece of fiber on the short end, adding on to it as he wrapped. He was fashioning a sturdy snare as Ben watched in amazement.

"Who are you?" Ben asked.

Chapter Five

The man didn't answer for a minute. Then he said, "I am a *mestizo*. Do you know what that is?"

"Yes. A person of mixed blood."

"Ah," the man said in his strange accent. "You put it politely. Some call me a 'breed' or a 'half-breed'. My mother was a Mexican and my father an Apache."

There was sadness in the old brown eyes of the man as he abruptly continued, "I wonder if you know what that is like? As a child, and then, as a man, to belong nowhere. Neither my mother's people nor my father's people wanted, nor accepted me fully. I was always on the outside, looking in. Finally, I grew tired of it; trying to belong where I was not wanted. For ten years I lived near a fort"—here he pointed to the southwest—"that the soldiers ran. I tried that.

"I worked for a good man who ran a store. I drove

his pack train, and brought in supplies. I learned his language and cared for his mules.

"But there, I did not belong, either, because one day soldiers in blue uniforms began to round up anyone of Apache blood to take them far away, to the east, where the sun comes from every morning. I did not want to go.

"My friend warned me and I slipped away and wandered for a while, then I came here. It was then that I gave up on trying to belong. Here, I belong only to myself."

"I can understand that," Ben said, thinking back to how he had felt unwanted at his own ranch after Ollie's marriage. And he'd known he was going to be even more unwelcome there when Lucy remarried.

The old man slowly continued talking, his hands steadily working at circling one set of fibers around the other.

"Although for many years I was angry at the unfairness of my lot in life, I no longer blame my parents. For a long time, I did.

"My beautiful mother and my handsome father did not think, with the passion of their love for each other, what consequences their love brought to their child—a *mestizo.*

"I was a man without a people. I was always straddling the line between two very different worlds and cultures—like a man trying to ride two horses at one time. Yes, that is a good picture of it, a man trying to ride two horses at one time."

He stopped winding to watch a hawk fly overhead. Ben stopped talking to watch too, because the hawk had something small—it looked like a mouse—in its talons.

They watched in silence until the hawk flew out of sight. Then the old man resumed talking.

"My parents did not stop to think that life would be hard for me; that I would not belong in either world, Mexican or Apache.

"Maybe in hundreds of years, when peoples have all mixed so much that no one remembers or cares who anyone is, it will be all right to be a *mestizo.*

"But for the first few, like me, it made my life very hard and I would not wish it on anyone else. That was, of course, many years ago. Perhaps it is better now.

"I learned to see inside both worlds, but from the outside only, like a ghost, always looking in."

Ben understood and felt sorry for the pain the old man had suffered.

The old timer stopped for a moment. "Forgive me, I am an old man and talk too much. As you see, I do not often have company." He chuckled, as if he were telling a secret joke only to himself.

"Go on," Ben said. "I am interested, and I do not think you talk too much." He found himself imitating the old man's formal way of talking. *Why was he doing that?*

"What brings you here to this lost place?" the old man said.

It was Ben's turn to chuckle at a secret joke. "I am

not lost. I meant to come here. I came here on purpose."

"To see me? How did you know I was here?"

"No, I didn't come to see you. I did not know you were here. I found the stairs . . . you . . . by accident."

He decided to be totally honest.

"I came here because I was disgusted. Disgusted with people and the way they are. People have lied about me. Stolen my land from me. Written false things to steal my land from me. I did not want to kill them in my anger, so I came here."

"Your God says 'Thou shalt not kill' I have heard. When I was younger I didn't understand that, but as I have grown older I can now see that there is great wisdom in that rule."

The old man nodded his head slowly as he spoke. He had finished the snare and laid it with the others beside him that were already completed.

Ben took his canteen off his shoulder, opened it, and offered the old man a drink.

The man shook his head, no. Ben took a drink, then closed up the canteen and laid it next to him.

"I've had a lot of bad luck in my life." Ben said, after a moment.

The old man's expression did not change, but he said slowly, "I do not believe so much—or maybe not at all—in this thing the white man calls luck.

"If a man runs out of water in the middle of the desert, is it bad luck? Or is it because he has neglected to learn where and how he can find water in the desert, before he began his journey?

"If a man runs a race and loses, it is just bad luck that he has lost? Or has he failed to think that if he is a big man, he should run the race that is short; for then he will beat the smaller man, who cannot keep up with the long strides of the tall man's legs?

"And if the man is short, does he think to run only in the long races, where the big man has to raise a large body and heavy bones off the ground and therefore tires quickly?

"In the short race, the big man always wins.

"In the very long race, the short man always wins. His small body can run for long periods of time without tiring. Is this luck, or being wise and smart?

"*It is wise to choose your races.* As a child, with my Apache relatives, I learned this by watching. Apache boys run many races as part of games they play.

Apache men are short, for the most part. Yet who can beat an Apache man in a race over a long distance? No one. He can often even keep up with a horse.

"No, I do not believe in luck, only in being wise.

"Tell me what these bad people you mentioned have done to you."

Ben said, "It may have been—be—hard to be a *mestizo.* But you are very smart. I have seen a lot of men race, but I never noticed what you have noticed. And you are right about the desert too."

When he was a kid back in Greenwater, he and Ollie had run lots of races too, as most of the boys did. He had won his share of them too. That was a long time ago.

He bent over toward the man and put out his hand. "What should I call you? My name is Benjamin Mitchell."

The old man took Ben's hand and shook it. His hand felt very dry—like paper skin and bones—very fragile.

"*Mestizo* is fine. Just call me *mestizo*. That is who and what I am. I have come to accept that."

"Call me Ben," Ben said.

He was curious. He wanted to talk some more to the smart old man. What would the man say about what had happened to Ben's land on Cedar Creek? Ben knew that Apaches didn't believe in the idea of owning land. But Mexicans did. Like the man said, two different cultures, *very* different in nearly every way.

He looked out. From the ledge, he could see that the old man had planted some crops, up safely away from the riverbed, on a flat bench area near the rock wall. The little "field" was hidden behind some trees and up on a dirt ledge where it prevented wildlife from getting to the crops too easily.

Smart.

It looked like corn and squash, and other things were growing in neat rows that had been watered recently. Each plant sat in a small round circle of wet dirt. It must be a lot of work carrying water to the crops from the river.

He saw an Apache-style waterproof basket on this

edge of the crops that the man must use to water the plants. It was sitting near the closest row of corn.

He looked back at where the *mestizo* sat on the blanket. Next to him on the blanket were two items that Ben knew were highly prized. They were a quiver and a bow case made of mountain lion skin. On the other side of the old man was a similar basket that he had made out of grasses by making coils.

The old man listened as Ben told the whole story of the ranch—Ollie and himself, Lucy and David Woolsey, the two lawyers—and, most of all, about the forgeries that said that he had sold his half of the ranch to Lucy.

The old man was silent.

It was a long time before he spoke.

Then he said slowly and carefully, "The Apache side of me says that you should go back and study. Learn the weakness of David and this Lucy and even David's father.

"You must ask him, and maybe yourself, why did David's father do this? You say you feel that he is not a bad man. What lie did Lucy tell this man to make him believe that he should lie and say that he was a witness when he wasn't?

"But most of all, you must study them all. Look for their weaknesses, and you may get your ranch back."

It seemed crazy—a crazy idea.

Ben was silent. To himself he was thinking, *"I will never go back. I'm going to be a hermit, like you."* He didn't say any of it out loud, but he thought it to himself.

"What of your mother and father? What about how they are feeling? What are they thinking of what has happened to you?" the old man asked.

"My parents are dead. I am alone in the world, like you. I'm afraid that if I go back, I'll end up killing somebody. I have a temper. I don't want to kill anybody. I left so that I didn't kill anybody. I'll be hanged for murder. The judge doesn't like me anyway."

The old man was silent, thinking.

He shook his head regretfully. "Still, I'm not sure that running away is the best answer for this particular problem. Instead, look for their weaknesses, like an Apache would do."

"What about your parents?" Ben asked. "Did you leave them behind?"

The old man looked up and gazed out across the canyon without talking.

Ben worried that he had hurt the old man's feelings. But then the man said, "They were dead long before I came here. Many times, the Mexicans and Apaches, my own peoples, they fight each other. It was a bad time for me. It was a long, long time ago and a long, long way from here."

The old man pointed south, then put his hand down.

The old man was tired, Ben could see.

"Wait here," Ben said. "I'll be right back." He got up and walked back on the ledge and down the rock stairs, got some things, and returned.

Ben handed the *mestizo* a half a pound of coffee, flour, potatoes, a few onions, and some bacon. Ben had made a bundle using his one extra blue shirt.

"Here, I brought you a present."

"Thank you," the man said. He was too proud to open the gift in front of Ben, but Ben knew that the minute Ben left, the old man would open it. He had a look on his face of fond appreciation, and Ben knew the *mestizo* was pleased.

"What will you do now?"

"I'm going to ride west, downriver, down the canyon," Ben said.

The old man chuckled. "Shall I wish you luck, then?"

Ben smiled at him. "No, that won't be necessary. I think I am going to try to think like you and believe the way you do. Try to use my brains. Maybe that way, I won't need luck."

"Soon it will be too hot here in the canyon bottom," the old man said. "So hot in the sun that a man wouldn't be able to touch metal without feeling pain. I will move, as I do each year, to a brush shelter up there," he pointed upward in back of himself, "back a ways from the rim of the canyon. Each year, I hope that the afternoon rains will come and care for my crops. Sometimes they do, sometimes they don't. That is all right. It is nature's way."

Ben shook the *mestizo's* hand.

With great difficulty, the *mestizo* got to his feet and went into the small dwelling behind him. He returned, after a long time, with a small package made out of what looked like rabbit furs sewed together into a pouch.

"You have been very generous," the *mestizo* said.

"Here is a small gift in return. I hope it will be useful." He handed the rabbit fur package to Ben.

Ben said, "Thank you."

The old man said, *"Adios,"* as Ben got up to leave. Ben knew that that translated to "Go with God."

"Adios," Ben said in return, and left. Walking along the ledge to the stairs, he climbed down and walked toward Paddy.

When he reached Paddy he opened the package the *mestizo* had handed him. Inside was a pair of Apache-style moccasins. They were the kind that covered your legs all the way up to the knees, to protect the wearer's legs from prickers and cactuses. They were made wide enough to wear on the outside of trousers so the trouser legs could be tucked comfortably inside.

They were beautifully made, a present from the *mestizo*. They looked like they were the perfect fit. Gently, he folded them and put them back inside the rabbit fur pouch. He then put the rabbit fur package in his saddlebag, and mounted up. Flies were bothering Paddy and he was swishing his tail back and forth to keep them away.

"Come on, Paddy, let's go," he said, adding, "Let's get you away from the flies."

He headed Paddy headed west, downriver.

Use your brains, and maybe you won't need luck, he reminded himself, as he rode off along the edge of the green river.

Chapter Six

He made his way downstream, still thinking about the old man. Even though the *mestizo* had lived alone in the cliff dwelling for so long, he seemed happy enough. He seemed very, very old.

The old man was right. The days were getting hotter here in the canyon. And he was right about the rain too.

In the afternoon, gray thunderclouds gathered and the downpours that resulted could water the old man's crops, or wash them away. The crops were as safe as the old man could make them, up high like they were, away from the river. Ben hoped that the crops would be all right up there. He had faith that the old man knew from experience what to do.

I wish I had had some more clothing to leave him, he said to himself. The old man's hand-sewn clothing was threadbare. Although he had never been inside,

Ben guessed that in the interior of the rock-walled house there were other items of clothing equally as old.

The next afternoon it rained, and he noticed something as he rode with his rainslicker on: it was the side creeks emptying into the bigger canyon that carried most of the muddy red silt into the main river of the canyon.

He noticed something else. When it was a hot day, like now, the canyon bottoms looked like they were steaming after it rained. White clouds of moisture, similar to fog, rose straight up. It was quite an amazing sight to see.

As he rode, he had time to think, and he realized that the *mestizo* had pointed, not toward the direction that Ben himself had come down into the canyon, but behind himself.

That must mean that behind the old man, somewhere, was another way up out of this canyon, behind him, to the north. Ben had come upon the canyon from the south.

The old man must know a way to get up the other side—the northern side.

He crossed back to the other side of the river, doing the same thing that he had done to cross over to the *mestizo's* side, carrying the provisions over, and then going back and bringing Paddy. Now he was back on the south side of the river; the side where he had come down.

He traveled, grateful that so far he had not come to

a place where he and Paddy would be blocked from going further.

He spent the night on a spot where the river in past years had flooded and made a wide flat place.

A half hour after dawn the next morning, as he rounded a bend in the river, he was surprised to come upon a pack of wild burros. It was difficult to count, because they all scurried off as quickly as they could, but he guessed that there were fifteen to twenty jennies and one jack.

He knew quite a bit about burros.

His father had once told him that the jack rules the herd. Two jacks, his father had said, will fight to maintain rulership. The fight, he said, sometimes lasts for days, and the loser must leave the herd.

How did this bunch of wild burros get here, so deep in this maze of isolated canyons? They took off ahead of him in a noisy, braying bunch, rounding the next bend and running out of sight.

He saw later where they had left the main canyon and gone off up a side canyon. Perhaps they knew ways that he was unaware of to get up and down the canyon walls.

He remembered another thing that his father said. His father always said that burros can fight off mountain lion attacks better than deer, antelope, horses, or cattle. They had tough skin. Their heavy hair made it tough for the teeth of the lion to pierce it, and their teeth and hooves were remarkably quick, so that a lion soon learned it would be wiser to choose a different prey.

Not to mention the horrible loud honking bray that burros were capable of making, he joked to himself. That would scare off most predators, he thought, smiling.

His father, in his youth, had done his share of prospecting further south in the Vulture Mountains of Arizona with a burro. His father had always been fond of burros. After his father had given up on prospecting, he used burros to pack in supplies to Arizona Territory from New Mexico. He brought in flour, grain, and salt to Websterville.

His father, Morgan Mitchell, had met his mother, Emily Ann, in New Mexico on one of his trips. After they were married, he returned with her to Greenwater, Texas—near where he had been born—settled on a wide grassy strip of land near Wisdom Creek, and began ranching.

Even though most ranchers didn't bother with burros, his own father had kept a few on the Texas ranch "to pack wood and to move hay," he said. Ben had suspected that they were there mostly for sentimental value.

His mother had always said that she didn't care much for the sound of a burro's braying, but she said it with a smile. Websterville had been a "one-horse town" when his father had worked there, Ben knew. In fact, it was his father's stories about his younger years living and working in Websterville that had prompted Ollie and Ben to come west and try their luck there.

His father said that when the mining craze was at

its height, there was an unspoken town rule: no one mentioned the shootings in the saloons the night before. When there was a shooting, the sheriff came right away and held an informal inquest right then, in the saloon. The guilty person or persons were taken away to jail, and the innocent went on about their business the next morning as if nothing had happened.

At that time, his father said, it was also an unspoken rule that you never asked questions concerning anybody's name if you wanted to live another day.

When Ben had first arrived, he found the number of bulletholes in the walls and floors of one particular bar—the Long Horn—unsettling. He and Ollie rarely went there. The town had quieted down since, but some of the "wildness" of its past still existed.

Before this, Ben had never had anything against Websterville. It had seemed to be—was—a nice town—at least, until Lucy arrived. James Magee ran the livery stable and Mrs. Mercer ran the hotel. Shorty Squibb was the sheriff. Good people. He hoped that they didn't believe lying Lucy. That's what he should call her from now on, Lying Lucy!

Chapter Seven

He had gone a long way down the canyon over a lot of rock. Around mid-morning, he got down off Paddy to check Paddy's horseshoes. They were fine.

As he put Paddy's last hoof down, his eye was drawn to a pile of dull, pale orange rock that had fallen over the years. The pile of rock was up against a yellow limestone or sandstone rock wall. As Ben looked up to the top of the canyon wall, he saw that weathering at the top, along an orange layer high up on the rim, had eroded that layer into a dangerous looking pile of rocks of all sizes that were just teetering on the edge.

Wind, water, rain, or something had undermined the various size rocks and boulders. They were just sitting up there, unattached, waiting for something to allow them to fall. Some of them had already made it down here to the bottom, and lay about, making piles of boulders of all sizes.

He decided to keep an eye out for snakes, and made a note to himself to get out of this area right away.

Suddenly, something, he didn't know quite what it was, caught his eye. Something out of place.

Too brown. Too brown to be near—or actually under—orange-colored rock.

He debated, should he go and look and see what it was? Or use common sense, and get out of here. Curiosity drew him cautiously closer.

Yes! He was right. It *was* a piece of leather.

He dropped the reins on the ground in front of his horse. Paddy was trained to stand there when Ben did that. He took a minute to look around and watch the scrubby trees and shrubs to see if there was any sign of breeze or wind, but everything was still and quiet.

He looked, but up at the top, there was no sign of windy conditions either. He went forward cautiously. If what he thought was right—

He was.

It was the old, old remnant of a man's brown leather boot, split and cracked and deteriorated, sticking out from under one of the dull orange rocks. Almost unrecognizable.

You could still make out the shape of the heel and sole, and a small portion of the bootleg.

It was what was left of a man.

The boulder in the center of the pile, about the size of a bushel basket, had been big enough to have done the job. It had hit the man's head or back, Ben wasn't sure. It looked like it had fallen on the unsuspecting man from up above. The man never had a chance, probably; the rock had fallen silently down. Maybe he had felt the horror of looking up at the last second, other rocks quickly following.

It looked like additional rocks, larger and smaller, had fallen on the man then, or later. The body was mostly buried now.

Ben picked up enough of the rocks and moved them aside to reveal what was left of a very old body. What he saw next put his heart to pounding, because if a similar fate met with him, it might be another ten or twenty years before *his* body was found.

Tooled into the black leather holster of the gun on the left side of the body—it was an old Colt—was a very faint set of initials which had once been painted red. Now, there were only the faintest traces of red. With difficulty, he made out two initials: S. L.

This was the body of the Lost Prospector!

Samuel Logan.

Here you are, Ben thought, *here you are in this canyon.* Ten years he had lain here. Undiscovered. *Is this how I want to end up?* Here, in a maze of canyons and side canyons, each one like so many others, with no landmarks to help identify which one was the one where Samuel Logan lay for all eternity, alone.

The belt buckle that had once been silver was black with tarnish. The belt was in bad shape, but Ben managed to slide off the holster with the initials. The Colt was still inside the holster.

He got up, walked over to Paddy, and put the Colt

and the holster in one of Paddy's saddlebags. He felt bad for the man.

He walked over to the body. As he knelt again, he noticed that there was something showing under a rock near what had been the man's pantleg.

It was a small leather pouch with rawhide string ties. He picked it up and opened it. In it he found about twenty gold nuggets. A couple of them were quite large and must be worth a pretty penny.

He would never rob a body, but he figured that if he sent them to Websterville, the judge could send the nuggets to Samuel's next of kin. By chance he had solved the mystery of what had happened to the Lost Prospector!

He found himself talking to the man lying there, dead for ten years, as if the man were listening. He didn't talk out loud, but he said it to himself.

"I'll take this holster back to Websterville, so that the people there know what happened to you. And I'll see that the nuggets get to your closest family member. That's about all I can do for you now."

In one way, Samuel Logan had been lucky. The rocks had covered enough of his body so that animals had not been able to get at it and tear it apart.

Ben spent some time finishing covering the body with the orange rocks that had fallen nearby. When the body was completely covered, Ben took off his hat, and said a few words he remembered from the Bible. He didn't remember the words exactly, but he said them as close to what he remembered as he could. It was his favorite part of the Bible: "The Lord is my shepherd; I shall not want. He maketh me to lie down in green pastures; he leadeth me beside the still waters. He restoreth my soul. He leadeth me in the paths of righteousness. Yea, though I walk through the valley of the shadow of death, I will fear no evil, for You are with me." He paused, because he had forgotten the next part, but then he continued, "Lord, if it pleases you, may this man, Samuel Logan, dwell in your house—the house of the Lord—forever."

Then he said, "Amen," and after a few seconds added, *"Adios"*. Go with God.

He put his hat back on.

Last, he searched until he found two scraps of cedar, and cutting a few strips off a small piece of rawhide he had in his saddlebag, he tied the leather strips together and then lashed the cedar together to make a small crude cross. He stuck the cross in the pile of rocks.

Paddy stamped his foot.

"Just a minute," Ben said, taking one last look at the newly constructed grave. The man had spent ten years alone out here. Paddy could sacrifice one more minute. Ben bowed his head, was silent for a moment, and then said, aloud to the man inside the pile of rocks that was now his grave: "Don't feel too bad, Mr. Logan. In some ways, we all die alone."

He got back up on Paddy. But this time, he turned Paddy back, back the way they had come. Up the canyon, eastward, back toward the place where he hoped he and Paddy could climb back up, out of the deep canyon in the earth.

Seeing that lonely body had made Ben come to a decision. He didn't want to end up like that. That was all his foolish anger—riding off in a huff—would accomplish. He was going back to try to get his ranch back.

He rode for a while, still seeing that boot sticking out from under that pile of rocks in his mind, not thinking consciously about anything else, just the sadness of it.

He rode some more, sighing. Paddy seemed to sense Ben's mood and walked along quietly also.

I want to get that ranch back, he thought. But how?

Paddy moved steadily beneath him, his muscles making their familiar rhythm under Ben's body.

The thought occurred to Ben that you can't be beaten if every time you get knocked off your feet and land in the dirt, you get up.

Sam Logan was down, but he, Ben, was still standing up. Maybe that was what courage was. Even if you've got a hole in one of your socks, and had done some mighty foolish things, such as trusting a woman that your gut feelings told you not to, and leaving important papers in her bedroom. He should have used his brains. Then he wouldn't be in this mess.

But he had come to a decision. He knew that he didn't want to live and die alone out here as Mr. Logan did; he was going to try and follow the *mestizo's* advice. His wild anger was gradually turning into resolution; a firm resolution to change things.

But how? How was he going to do it?

He had no idea.

But he did know a few things that had to be done, anyway. And he had to go back to Websterville to do them. Back in Websterville, he would give the nuggets either to his lawyer Ephram, or to Judge Colby. Neither one was on his list of favorite people right now, but they were at least honest. And he would give the holster to them to prove that his story was true. No. Instead he would give the holster and nuggets to Sheriff Squibb.

This time, at least, the people in town would *have* to believe him.

As he rode east up the canyon, he thought about Samuel Logan's two mules. They had returned to Websterville. How had they ever done that?

It was amazing that they had found their way up out of this long, deep canyon and then all the way back to Websterville. He wondered if they went the way he had come or had found another way. No one would ever know.

It rained once in the afternoon as he made his trip back up the canyon, and he put on his slicker. He saw a coyote as he traveled back the way he came. The weather was sunny as he passed by the *mestizo's* home on the way back out of the canyon. He left Paddy on the south side, crossed the river, and went up the stairs to the rock house on the ledge, but it was empty.

Had he already moved to the top of the canyon? Ben didn't think so. Not yet. It was still pleasant in the canyon, for the most part. Probably out checking his snares. He looked out over the ledge to see if the man was down below watering his crops.

There was no sign of him.

He left a small amount of coffee wrapped up well in a piece of rawhide in front of the rock house and drew a picture in the dirt of a stick figure going up a wall to tell the old man that he was leaving the canyon.

He drew it carefully near the rock wall by the house where it would be out of the rain as much as possible, in case the man didn't come back for a while.

He waded back across the river for the last time, and started Paddy on the journey to the place where he and Paddy had come down into the canyon.

Today, the river was red. The trip back to the place where the trail upward began was quiet. This time, he and Paddy would be going up.

Ben thought back to the trip down into the canyon. When he was leading Paddy down, one of the dangers was that Paddy would stumble and fall forward and send him over the edge.

Going up, that would not be the worry. Tomorrow, he would have a different cause for concern; that Paddy would fall backward, pulling them both over the edge.

He thought again about how good Paddy had been going down. He hoped that the claybank gelding would be as good going up.

They camped for the night at the bottom of the trail. In the morning, when Paddy was fresh, they would start up. He was glad, in a way, to be going back to Websterville. Even though he had started out angry and wanting to be by himself for a while, he had found out something about himself on this trip.

He wanted—needed—to be with people, as rotten as they could sometimes be. Maybe he didn't want or need a crowd of people, but he wanted to be with a few of them at a time. Good people. It was too lonely for him, here in the wilderness. If he got the ranch back, he would telegraph back to Texas and see if he could get Miguel to come back.

He had a new understanding of why men clustered together in towns, even when there was so much space available, and even a little understanding of why lonely cowboys went to town as often as they could. They wanted companionship. So did he.

His anger had faded somewhat on this solitary journey. At least he had cooled down from his previous rage. The journey had accomplished that, if nothing else.

He only wished that there were more available women around. There still were so few out here. Maybe it had caused Ollie to be too hasty and make a bad choice.

Ben had found out one thing about himself: He was not cut out to be a hermit.

An expression that his mother used to use came back to him as he made camp for the night. It was not exactly about running away from problems, but on a similar subject. She used to say, "You can't go through life with a cloth bag over your head". She meant that she didn't want her two sons going through life ignoring problems—blinding themselves to what was really going on. Pretending that bad things didn't exist, by ignoring them. In a way, maybe that was what he had tried to do, by riding away.

The morning trip up the canyon was nerve-racking, but uneventful. As he had going down, he gave Paddy water from his hat from time to time.

It was early afternoon when he rounded the last bend and reached the switchback area right at the top of the canyon. One last great effort and he and Paddy were up out of the canyon!

Now they would be heading south toward Websterville. It was late afternoon when the shot came out of nowhere.

Chapter Eight

If it weren't for the fact that Ben reached forward at that very instant to pat Paddy fondly on the neck, he would have been dead.

Instead, the shot went across his back rather than into his heart. It felt like a hot branding iron had been run across his back. Lucy and David! was his first thought.

The world went light gray, then faded to blackness in front of his eyes. He was unconscious as he fell from Paddy's back.

When he woke, he was lying on his stomach. He saw that he was in a small dark rock-walled room with no windows. He turned his head on the pillow slowly, side to side, looking as much as he could around the room. He could not see directly behind him.

Only a single, soot-blackened and battered tin oil lamp was burning. It was on a crude pine table on the right side of the bed. There was one low doorway to the right.

The walls were made of brownish-yellow rock. Ben saw a large shiny black spider sitting on a rock slab jutting out on the wall a few inches above him, close to his head. He could make out the telltale red hourglass shape on its underside.

A black widow spider.

He wanted something to kill the spider with, but he found when he tried to pick up his head, he was too weak to get up and kill it anyway.

There was nothing else in the room except a crude-looking pine chair next to the bed on the left, as least that he could see. On the right was the table with the oil lamp burning. There was nothing else on the table that would help kill the spider.

He had to put his head back down. He was seeing pink, green, and blue shiny-colored spots in front of his eyes, just from the effort of lifting his head. He thought he was going to faint.

He rested a minute or two, then slowly picked up his head and tried to look up again at the rock where the spider had been.

The spider had disappeared, but that didn't make him feel any better. He felt around under the sheets, but his gun, and indeed his shirt, were gone off his body. He managed to lift the sheet and look under his arm where he saw that although his boots were off, his dusty black trousers were still on.

He took a look and wryly decided that he didn't have to worry much about dirtying the sheets on the bed, as they were about the oldest and dirtiest yellowed sheets—both top and bottom—he had ever seen. An equally dirty black, red, and yellow Indian blanket was neatly folded over the back of the chair next to the bed.

Even in this dire situation, he had to chuckle at the thought of how his mother would react if she ever saw him in such a dirty bed. Picking up the sheet as best he could, he raised himself up painfully by the elbows, then looked down at himself again. He saw that there was a—miraculously—clean, large, very white bandage around his upper chest.

He looked down at the bandage, holding up the dirty brown-looking sheet. It looked like a good job.

He heard footsteps and the faint rustling of clothes, and quickly laid himself down and pretended to be asleep.

A surprisingly gentle man's voice said, "Don't need to bother to pretend to be asleep. I'm not going to hurt you. Heard you talkin' to yourself from the other room." You said, "My mother would have a fit if she saw these dirty sheets," the man said. He chuckled. "So might mine 'ov."

Ben raised himself up again as best he could and turned his head and looked. He had had no idea that he was talking out loud to himself. He wondered how often he did that. Probably more than he realized. He managed slowly and painfully to roll over onto his side to look at the man.

The man, who had entered the room carrying a tin cup with a spoon in it, was a medium-sized person with an oval face and small pug nose. His hair, worn long down past his shoulders, was an odd shade, somewhere between light brown and blond, with a grayish cast. He had a long but thin handlebar mustache, and was dressed in dusty black clothing. He looked young. Eighteen or nineteen. Maybe a bit older. It was hard to tell.

"Bad habit, a man gets into, talking to himself," Ben said. "I didn't even know that I said that out loud."

"Maybe, like me, you been alone too much."

Ben nodded his head up and down, very slowly, in agreement. Too fast, and he knew the spots would appear again before his eyes.

"How did I get here?" Ben asked. "How is my horse?"

The man put the tin cup and spoon on the table near the lamp and came forward. He picked up the folded blanket on the back of the chair and folded it to make a pillow out of it. He picked up Ben's head and put the "pillow" underneath, then helped Ben prop himself partially up, using the blanket as a backrest.

Moving the chair around to the same side as the table, the man sat on the chair near the small bed. Then the stranger picked up the tin cup and the spoon off the table next to the bed. Parts of the pine chair still had bark on it, Ben saw.

The stranger dipped the spoon into the cup and then put the spoon to Ben's mouth.

Soup, just the right temperature—warm and soothing—was in his mouth, gliding down his dry throat.

"I brought you," the man answered. "Just call me Doc."

As he looked at the man feeding him, all of a sudden Ben was aware of something he had seen but had not registered until then. The stranger spoon-feeding him had a professional gunfighter's rig on. His gun was tied down. It was a fancy Colt. One of the best-looking guns Ben had ever seen. It had ornate silver fancy scrolls and feathers engraved on it, not like the plain Navy Colt that Ben used.

Something about it, and the man facing him, made Ben know he was lucky to be alive. Only his affection for Paddy had saved him. He had leaned forward at just the right moment.

The man gave him another spoonful of soup. Ben thought that the soup was the best thing he had ever eaten. He was very grateful. It was soothing to his very dry throat.

"Your horse is fine. I been takin' care of him real good. No need to worry about that. Even curried him this morning. Used my own personal comb," the man said, grinning.

"Where did you find me?" Ben asked, wondering at the same time how there could have been more than one person in the vast, lonely desolate area that they were both in; the shooter, and this doctor.

"I didn't find you," the man said, and Ben recognized the regret in the man's voice.

"I was the one shot you," Doc continued.

"You shot me? Then why . . ." Ben said, looking around at the room.

What he was asking, was, if you're the one who shot me, why have you saved me?

The man knew what Ben meant.

"Shot you by mistake," the man said. "Thought you were the lead man—the tracker—for a posse."

"A posse? Up here?"

The man shook his head regretfully, the light hair brushing back and forth over his shoulders as he turned his head. "Long story," he said.

Ben looked around the room. "I got time, if you do."

The doctor chuckled. "All right." He gave Ben a third spoonful of soup.

"No names, agreed?"

"Agreed," Ben said.

The man continued to feed Ben as he told his story.

"My father was a doctor back in New Mex . . . back east aways. I lost both my parents to cholera when I was twelve. Been on my own since then. Scrounged around till I was about sixteen, and then I got what I thought was an honest job.

"I worked for a year and a half on a ranch for a cattleman. Tole me he was banking my pay for me. Savin' it for me. When I wanted to leave, and asked for my back pay—the pay the man had agreed to when he hired me—the man double-crossed me. Said he didn't owe me anything. I was mighty mad, but I left empty-handed.

"I went to another town, and apprenticed to a doctor I knew slightly. When I had the money, I bought a gun and did a mite of practicin'. Then I went back and confronted the cheatin' scoundrel.

"All I got to say is, I got my money. Then I went back and worked again for the doc. Long about when I was nineteen, I got in with a bad crowd. Hung around the saloons, drinkin' with them. About that time a banker from two towns over came to us with a scheme. Seemed like it would be a hoot—a fun thing—at the time. We was to go in with handkerchiefs over our mouths and *pretend* to rob his bank real early in the morning, when no one was around town.

"We were supposed to leave the money in a secret place in the bank, hidden under a floorboard near the back door. Then we was to ride out of town with sacks filled with newspapers cut to look like money. Me 'n two of my friends thought that sounded like a hilarious joke!

"Then, after we left, the banker was to run and get the sheriff. The banker was supposed to say that we rode off in the other direction than we really did. We was really riding west and the banker was to say we rode east. We were supposed to meet the banker the next day and divide up the money.

"Banker double-crossed us, needless to say. Tole the sheriff the real way that we went. Even went *with* the posse. It was him that shot my friends Johnny Green and Jim Shaker. I was the only one who got away. Johnny and Jim were only sixteen years old. Mostly my fault, I guess. I was the oldest and should have known better. Johnny and Jim were just kids.

That was about eight months ago. Been on the dodge ever since. Can't say as I like the life much. This here's been my hideout off and on, since then."

The ominous thought filled Ben's mind that the outlaw would never let Ben go, now that he knew where the hideout was.

The man knew what Ben was thinking. The soup was gone, and the outlaw got up and put the cup and spoon on the table. He pulled the chair a small distance away from the bed and sat back down in it, crossing his legs by putting one leg across the top of the other.

Ben looked up. The spider reappeared, then disappeared in between two rocks in the wall before he could say anything.

The outlaw looked down at his lapel and brushed off some dust. "Don't worry. I was thinkin' on leavin' here, anyway. Won't say where I'm goin'," the man chuckled, "but it's gonna be somewheres where water ain't so hard to come by. Gettin' tired of luggin' water so far. This here's a big country. Figger somewheres," he waved his hand around in a circle to show a big space far away, "out there, there's a place that needs a doc. I spent that time apprenticed to Doc Ka—" he caught himself just in time, "to a doctor. Learnt about all there is to know between that, and' watchin' my pa all those years."

He seemed to be studying one of the rocks in the wall, but Ben knew that the doc was thinking to himself.

"Well, I think that nursin' you back from the dead," he chuckled, "showed me that I like it a lot better savin' people than hurtin' them. A life of crime ain't for me. I ain't got the brains for that, obviously."

He grimaced. "Would have liked to get that banker, though, before I moved on to a 'purer' life."

Something about the story jogged a faint memory of something—a rumor Ben had once heard, that he'd dismissed at the time. "Banker wouldn't have the name of Charlie Banks, by any chance, would he?"

The stranger raised his eyebrows. "Why yes, he would."

"Charlie Banks died from cholera down in Websterville, 'bout six months ago. I remember hearing vague rumors about his past, but I never believed them—until now," Ben said.

Ben was going to add that "he did me a favor once," but he thought better of it. Strangely enough, that was true. When Mrs. Winslow was widowed suddenly, he went and asked Charlie if he would give the widow a "seed" loan. Charlie had said yes, for some reason. Ben had always attributed it to kindness. Now he wondered. In fact, that Websterville bank was now owned by his own enemy, John Woolsey, David's father.

Life had its little ironies like that, he guessed. He, himself, was no smarter than "Doc" or Ollie. He would never have guessed that good old Charlie Banks had a crooked past.

That was one thing about the west. Out here, you never knew. People judged you for how you acted today, here and now. It was considered impolite to question anyone's past.

"I can't believe I missed you. I never missed before when I shot anybody," Doc said. "Missing you has changed my life."

It almost changed mine permanently, Ben thought to himself.

He could see the dark humor of the situation. Here he was, depending on his almost-killer, to save him. He suspected that "Doc" had done a good job on his back wound. It didn't hurt, unless he moved, which, apparently, he couldn't—very fast, at least.

Ben chatted with the man a few minutes longer, then he grew tired. Doc could see that he was tired, turned the oil lamp to low, and left, leaving Ben in almost total darkness.

He thought about asking "Doc" to look for and kill the spider, but he felt stupid and foolish asking it, so he didn't. A little worried, he slept.

When he woke, the oil lamp was on and the man's gentle hands were touching his shoulder, urging him to wake up. "I need to roll you over and put a new dressing on that wound."

With the outlaw-doctor's help, Ben rolled to his side and propped himself up on one elbow so that the dressings could be unwound.

It hurt. The doc, seeing that, pushed the rolled-up blanket under Ben's armpit to help take the pressure off his chest muscles.

"It's only a flesh wound. You were real lucky," the

doc said. Ben wondered what the *mestizo* would have to say about that.

The doctor tended to the wound, putting some salve on it that looked suspiciously like horse liniment. It was some kind of greasy stuff, at any rate.

Doc put the tin container back on the table beside the bed, and put the lid back on. Then he rebound the wound, wrapping clean dressing around Ben's chest.

Neither man spoke. The doctor seemed worried that he had spoken so freely before. Ben could understand why. He only hoped the doctor hadn't changed his mind.

Once again the doctor knew what Ben was thinking. "I haven't changed my mind, if that's what you're wondering." He finished, tucking the last of the wrap inside the cloth, and removed the blanket from under Ben's armpit. Ben lay back down.

"You think your stomach could hold some deer stew?"

Ben said, "It could and be dang glad to get it."

Doc chuckled. "Be back in a minute with some, then."

Ben was glad when the man went out. He looked for the spider, and managed to reach over and grasp the round tin that the liniment came in. He planned, aimed, and smashed the round tin down on the spider, which was only about eight inches from his head.

The tin made a loud noise as it hit the rock. He got it! He was very relieved.

The doc stuck his head in the door, concerned.

"Killing a spider," Ben said. He put the tin back down on the table, and lay back down, exhausted.

"Oh," Doc said, and disappeared again.

It was getting awkward.

Ben wondered how soon—and if—he would be free to go. He tried to sit up, but the effort was too great. He fell back, and this time, the pain was bad, because he had pulled muscles near the wound.

It would be a few days until he was well enough to—well, do whatever he had to do. If he had a few meals, he felt that his strength would come back.

When the doctor came back with the deer stew, Ben ate it with great appreciation. It did make him feel stronger.

Chapter Nine

After Ben ate the deer stew, he fell asleep, and it wasn't until the next morning that he woke up. If the outlaw had entered the room to check on Ben during the night, Ben had no memory of it. He had slept like a log, Ben thought to himself.

The doc entered the room. "Sorry, but it's deer stew again for breakfast," the doc said. He was carrying the same battered tin bowl with him as last night, but it had been washed and dried since then. Ben wondered how far the doc had to go for water.

He said "Thanks," and this time, he fed himself.

The man said, "I tole you my story. What's yours? I can't help wonderin' what you're doin' up here, alone. I thought I was the only man in forty miles in any direction."

Ben thought about the *mestizo,* but didn't break the rhythm of spooning out the deer stew. "It's sure a lonely place up here," he said, as he finished chewing a chunk of deer meat. "Have to agree with you on that."

He decided that honesty was the best policy and told the man about Ollie, Lucy and all that had happened. In both their stories, they had one thing in common. They had had to deal with rascals and crooks. They had each dealt with it in their own way.

And Doc was a lot younger when he had run into his first crook. Ben had to admire that the outlaw, on his own since he was only knee-high to a grasshopper, had gone back to confront his crooked employer. It was very courageous, even if a bit foolhardy.

In fact, that was what Ben planned to do, once he was better. He told the man how he was going back to confront Lucy and the two Woolseys. He didn't mention the *mestizo*, or the fact that the Woolseys ran the bank and the land office.

"I think now that I was wrong to run away like that," Ben said.

"I don't know about that," the outlaw said, to Ben's surprise. "Maybe you did right. Look what happened to me. Don't know if I done the right thing neither."

Does anyone ever know? Ben thought to himself. *You just do the best you can at the time.*

Doc didn't mention it, but there was probably a bounty on his head. That was really why the outlaw had shot first and asked questions later. Doc had said he thought it was a posse—and maybe he was telling the truth—but he probably purposely omitted the part that he thought Ben could have been a bounty hunter.

He didn't want Ben to know that there was a price on his head in case Ben got any ideas, obviously.

That was the last thing on Ben's mind. He just wanted to get out of here in one piece and back to Websterville to solve his own problems. Without letting on about the bounty business, he tried to say that to the outlaw. "I just want to go about my own business, Doc. I have no interest in adding to your problems."

"I know that. That's why you're still alive. Could tell you're a good person by what you talked about in your sleep, when you were first shot. By the way, what's that stuff in your saddlebags? There's a rotten old holster and gun."

Ben decided that the truth could only help him here. Obviously, the outlaw had gone through the saddlebags. He would have found the small sack of gold.

If he was going to take it, he already had.

If not, there was no reason to lie.

He told the story of finding the body of Samuel Logan, and about the gun and the gold.

The outlaw said, "How come his body wasn't all torn apart by coyotes, wolves, and vultures?"

Ben explained how the rockfall had covered all but a boot.

"That's an interesting story. It makes me realize. . . ."

Ben said, "It made me realize the same thing. Dying alone like that. . . ."

Both men knew. Both men had chanced the same thing, but for different reasons.

Both of us know, Ben thought, *that it's time to go back to civilization.*

He felt that he and the doctor-outlaw had reached a kind of wary friendship.

But he wouldn't breathe a real sigh of relief until the stranger had let him ride away, and until he was sure that there would be no surprise bullet in his back.

Chapter Ten

He was the one who was surprised. On the fourth morning he felt strong enough to sit up slowly and pull and push his legs around and down off the bed.

Next to the bed on the chair was a dark brown clean shirt. The doc had obviously left it for him to put on. He did, slowly and painfully, putting his arms in the shirt and then buttoning the shirt one button at a time. There was no sign of the old light brown shirt with the bullethole in the back.

He took his time and slowly got to his feet. He was woozy, but he managed to walk across the dirt floor of the small room to the doorway.

In front of him was another small, rock-walled room. There was a very small round potbellied stove near the left wall, and a table on the right wall. There were no windows in the walls, and as a result the room was very dark. The only light that came into the room was through the small leather-hinged door, which had been left open a crack, probably to let in a little fresh air.

Already he could feel that it was hot outside, as he walked toward the door. His back pained him somewhat as he moved, but it was bearable. Outside, he saw that only Paddy stood there. He was saddled and hitched to a small shrub near the doorway. He looked well-fed, and Ben could see that he had recently been curried. Ben's supply and saddlebags hung neatly from either side of the saddle. Paddy was ready to ride.

There was no sign of the doctor. His horse, and all his belongings were gone. He had left *first*. Ben let out a big sigh of relief. Not until that moment had he realized just how worried he had been that the man would change his mind about everything and kill Ben.

Paddy whinnied, and Ben slowly made his way over to the horse and patted him. "Glad to see you, boy." Paddy nuzzled Ben. More out of curiosity than anything, and not expecting to find the gold still there, he felt around in the saddlebag.

To his surprise, the gold *was* still there. Knowing Ben needed it to tell his story and be believed, the doctor had left the gold; even though Ben was sure Doc could have used it to get where he was going. The doctor was sending Ben a message. As different as they were, they were friends.

There was some additional irony in this trip, Ben thought to himself. He had come to the canyon area to be alone. But the canyons seemed to be getting somewhat crowded. They were no longer such an isolated place that no one went there. He had run across three people: two alive, and one dead.

It was time to head home. Back to Websterville. And face his problems head on. He went back inside, made his bed up, and straightened out what he could in the little hideout. When he went out, he carefully closed the small wooden door behind him.

Outside, he realized that the little dwelling he had been in for the last few days was one of the old Indian ruins that had been repaired, and a new log-and-dirt roof put on, probably by the doc. Doc had mentioned that he had been using this hideout for some months.

The effort of swinging up into the saddle on Paddy hurt his back, and so did riding, he found out. He had to rein Paddy in so the horse would go a little slower. It was hard to do, because Paddy was raring to go. He hadn't been ridden in a few days and was well rested. It was going to be a slow, painful ride back.

A mile or so outside of Websterville, Ben stopped to count his money. He had sixty-two dollars and a little change. Enough to move back into Mercer's Hotel for a while until he could think of what to do next.

And enough to have the doctor in Websterville check his wound.

Chapter Eleven

"Hey, Ben!" the sheriff, Shorty Squibb, yelled as Ben rode Paddy south through town toward Mercer's Hotel. He must have seen Ben through the sheriff's office window. He came hurrying out as Ben went by.

"Confound it, Ben, you know you caused an uprising in this here town? What did you mean, riding off like that? What were you thinking?" Out of breath, Shorty stopped a few feet away from Ben, who had reined in and stopped Paddy.

"What are you talkin' about?" Ben said, confused. "What uprising?" He dismounted, walked over, and tied Paddy to the hitching pole in front of Mercer's Hotel as Shorty began to speak.

Shorty followed him, rattling on so quickly that Ben couldn't get a word in. "Seems that you have a few more friends—people on your side—than you knew. You almost caused a riot! I thought that they were going to hang Judge Colby from the gallows when they heard that he didn't take your word fer what happened. Once word had spread, people got madder 'n a bunch of hornets that's done been got its nest split open. Got madder too as the afternoon wore on.

"Reckon Judge Colby was mighty surprised to see a bunch of people stormin' his house early that evenin'. Seems they tole him in no uncertain terms that you was a good guy! Tole him they knew you five years an' that *Lucy* was the stranger. Asked him what the heck was the matter with him.

"Tole him that the reason he didn't know you better was that you kept your nose clean—didn't do nothin' that would cause you to have to face him in court. Jeb Skeggs tole the judge rather loudly, as I recall, that it was you that arranged for him to get a load of lumber from up north when his house burnt that time, and Mrs. Winslow said that one time you talked the banker—you know, Charlie Banks, the one who died from cholera—into giving her a loan after her husband died.

"An' Buckshot Fenton said that one time when his son Brady was rebelling, you went and talked to him and got him to go a little easier on the son—said he was too strict with the kid—and Buckshot said that you were right; when he eased up on the kid, the kid turned out all right." Shorty stopped, out of breath.

Shorty was a small man, and but for his widely known skill with a shotgun, and knowledge of when and how to use both barrels, he might never have been able to carry off the sometimes dangerous job of being the sheriff in a mining settlement, even if it was turning slowly into a more ranching area. In addition to his shotgun skills, Shorty had never been accused of being short on brains.

The door of Ephram's law office, to the right of the courthouse, opened, and Ephram came hurrying out. He walked quickly over to where Paddy, the sheriff, and Ben were all standing, in front of Mercer's Hotel.

"Where in tarnation you been?" Ephram said, partly in annoyance, partly in embarrassment. Ben sensed that Ephram was on the defensive, maybe because of the town's possible reaction toward his poor handling of the case.

The thought had occurred to Ben on the ride back from Doc's shack that perhaps Ephram should have called some witnesses in the case. He guessed now that Ephram was thinking the same thing, or that someone in town had come right out and said that to him.

Maybe the outcome would have been different.

Ephram made an effort to show that he had tried. "Poor horseman that I am, with my bum leg and all, me an' a couple of your friends about rode out after you, but by that time you had disappeared into that bad canyon area up north, an' we lost yer tracks in the dust and dirt."

It showed Ben just how upset Ephram was that he had reverted to his old Tennessee way of talking. Usually, he tried to talk in a more educated way since he had studied and begun practicing law.

Ben knew that the reason that Ephram had become

a lawyer in the first place was that he had injured his leg during the War. The leg was pretty good now, and Ephram only limped when he was overtired. And he had been limping slightly as he came out of his office and over to Ben.

Ephram shook his head sadly in regret.

"Judge Colby said that it was too bad, but he can't change what he done:' What's done is done,' " Ephram said. "An' besides, the judge said, 'Ben Mitchell's gone, anyways. But now you're back."

Sheriff Squibb took off his hat and scratched his head in confusion, as if he as still thinking about it. "Law-wise, he could. But I don't think he wants to admit directly that he made a mistake. So I wouldn't count on it, Ben. Sorry."

The sheriff put his hat on and then walked away, returning to his office.

He had omitted giving Ben any warning as to Ben's behavior in town, and Ben knew and understood, and appreciated it. In effect, he was telling Ben that he knew Ben wouldn't make any trouble and would do the right thing.

Ben looked out at the far horizon for a minute thinking, then looked back at Ephram. "Don't worry, Ephram. I'll figure somethin' out."

Ephram looked at the back of the retreating sheriff and thought it over. "I know I don't need to tell you not to do anything crazy," Ephram said. "Let me know if I can be of any help."

Ephram started to walk away, and then came back. His shoulders were slumped, and he looked quite dejected. "This case has put quite a crimp in my business here in town. People blame me fer this. An' I got a wife an' two younguns to support. Put a blot on my record."

"I know," Ben said. "I'm sorry."

"I meant it," Ephram said. "Let me know if there's anything I can do. No charge."

He left, and returned to his office. Through the front window, Ben could see him sit down resignedly at his desk.

Ben remembered what was in his saddlebags, and he pulled the saddlebag off Paddy and walked over to the sheriff's office. On his way, he saw John, David's father, come out of the bank. John Woolsey's eyes widened in recognition, then he dropped his head, averting his eyes, so he would not have to look at Ben directly. *Good,* Ben said to himself, *let him be ashamed of what he's done!* It was obvious that John Woolsey was embarrassed to face him, as John turned quickly on his heel and went the other way.

Beside the Sheriff's office door, nailed to the wall, was a new poster with REWARD written in large letters at the top. Underneath, it said: *Three thousand dollars reward for any information leading to the arrest or apprehension of those involved in the killing of miners in the area surrounding Websterville, Arizona Territory. Contact Sheriff S. Squibb.* On the bottom it said *Miner's Association.*

Sheriff Squibb looked a little surprised when Ben walked in.

"Can I put this saddlebag on your desk, Sheriff?" Ben said, adding "I found something on my travels that I think you might be interested in."

Ben knew that Shorty was thinking that Ben had discovered ore.

He enjoyed seeing the surprised look on Shorty's face when he showed him the holster with the initials and the gun and the small pouch of gold. Even though his back was hurting, he chuckled at the expression of amazement on Shorty's face. In a few words, he told Shorty about finding the remains of Samuel Logan, and about what he wanted Shorty to do with the gold, and with the gun and holster.

"If Sam Logan's family wants the gun and holster, as well as the gold, I'll see that they get it. If I remember right, he had family down in Tucson. I'll just need to dig through a pile of paperwork to get their address. Then I'll see that a telegraph gets sent as soon as possible.

"Soon's I hear, I'll send these items right along. Family'll be happy to finally know what happened to Sam Logan."

Ben shook his head in agreement. He was glad that that errand was done. It was as if a load had fallen off his shoulders.

"Thanks, Shorty."

"No problem. Glad to do it. And Ben," Shorty said in a fatherly way, not quite looking Ben in the eye, as if he was embarrassed to say it out loud, "Glad yer back."

"Thanks. See you later," Ben said. He shut the door to the sheriff's office behind him as he left.

He walked over to Paddy and untied him and took him up the street to James Magee's livery stable, which was on the same side of the street as Mercer's Hotel and separated from Mercer's Hotel only by a small wooden Assay office building and the Gold Digger's Saloon.

Inside the stable, he found Jimmy Magee sitting in a chair reading a dime novel about the West.

He chuckled.

"Slow day today, Jimmy?"

Jimmy looked up.

Ben removed his saddlebags from Paddy.

"Hi, Ben. Sorry to hear about yer troubles," Jimmy said. "Here, give me those reins. I'll take good care of Paddy here for ya." He began walking away with Paddy.

"Give Paddy some grain, Jimmy," Ben said.

"No trouble. Will do that right away. A nice drink, and then a nice meal for him," Jimmy said, as if the horse were a person. "Even throw in a rubdown."

"Thanks. I'll be at Mercer's if you need me for anything."

"Don't you worry about a thing," Jimmy said.

Right. Don't worry about a thing, Ben said to himself.

He walked back on out into the bright sunlight, and then back to Mercer's Hotel. At the counter at the back of the room, he put his saddlebags and the two cloth bags down on the floor in front of the desk.

Inside, Mrs. Mercer came right over when she saw him.

"Sorry about what happened, Ben," she said. She was a large friendly plump woman who liked to joke that she had eaten "one too many cookies" in her life. She was about sixty and had had a lot of problems in her life, but she still managed to have a cheerful word for everyone. Ben suspected it was because she liked her life, running the hotel. She got to meet a lot of people. Mrs. Mercer liked people. He guessed a lot more than he, himself, did.

"Glad to have you back," she said. "Oh, I almost forgot. A letter came for you while you were gone. I left it behind the desk here."

With that, she reached down under the counter, picked up a letter, and handed it to him across the counter.

It was from Miguel. Someone had done the writing for him, obviously. It was written in a woman's hand.

Dear Ben,

Maria is writing this for me. I miss you and Oliver very much. You know you are family to me. Things are getting very modern down here in Texas. Fancy stoves and all. Texas isn't the same without you and Ollie. I don't care much for the new owners of the Wisdom Creek ranch where you used to live with your blessed parents—May they rest in peace. I have been staying with my niece, Maria, but most of my old friends have

*died or move away. It is most lonely now. I guess
I am getting old.*

Most affectionately,
Miguel

What he didn't say, and what was between the lines, Ben knew, was that Miguel wanted to come back to Websterville, but he was too proud to ask.

The letter's return address was a ranch near Wisdom Creek. The address was the Circle Bar Ranch, Greenwater, Texas, where Maria worked doing housework. The Barnes family owned the Circle Bar Ranch. They were the closest friends of his deceased parents. It was nice of the Barnes to take Miguel in.

Ben hoped that somehow, he would be able to write and send money for the old man to come soon. Miguel was family. He wanted Miguel back as soon as possible.

He put the letter in his pocket, picked up the pen, and wrote his name in the register.

"How long you gonna be stayin' this time?" Mrs. Mercer asked in her friendly manner that seemed to say "You're welcome to stay as long as you want." Her smile seemed real and welcoming.

"Don't know for sure, Mrs. Mercer. I'll be sure to let you know as soon as I know."

"You know you're welcome here as long as you want," she said.

He smiled at her. It was the first real smile that he had smiled in a long time. "I know that, Mrs. Mercer. You've got a good heart."

Now he had embarrassed her, and she busied herself

turning the hotel register around, and finding him a room key.

"Here, take this. Same room as before all right?"

She was asking him if he wanted a room facing the street, as he had had before, or one with the windows facing the back.

"Same room is fine," he said.

She handed the key to him, and he took it. He picked up his belongings, walked away from the counter, and over to the stairs on the right.

He went up the stairs and down the short hall and unlocked the door to room number 4.

He went in, walked over, and looked out the window. He was in the middle room in the front of the hotel. It looked out over the street.

He was directly opposite the sheriff's office-courthouse building. The Long Horn Bar was on the left of the courthouse, and Ephram Brazer's office on the right side. He could see all three clearly.

He went over and sat on the bed.

He took the letter out of his pocket and read it again. It was very like Miguel to get a woman to write his letter for him. Women liked Miguel, including his niece Maria. He was a gentleman. It was probably Mrs. Barnes who told Maria that it was all right if Miguel stayed on their ranch. Mrs. Barnes had always had a soft spot for Miguel. Who didn't? Everyone, in fact, who knew him—except Lucy.

He didn't even want to be reminded of her. He put the letter on the bed and left his hotel room, locking the door. He walked down the stairs and outside the hotel. Mrs. Mercer was not in the lobby, but a pretty woman was. She appeared to be looking around for a hotel clerk.

Mrs. Mercer was nowhere to be seen.

"Can I help you?" Ben asked politely from a distance, holding his black hat in his hands.

"I'd like to check in," the woman said. She was a medium-tall, thin, capable-looking woman. Her hands showed that she had done her share of hard work in the recent past.

She had on a light green calico dress with dark green trim. As he got closer, he could see her eyes were green and matched the dark green of the dress, and she had long dark eyelashes. Her hair was a dark, dark brown, almost black. It was shiny and very clean-looking, as if it had just been washed. Her nose was small and perfect.

"I'll go and fetch Mrs. Mercer." He circled widely around the woman and went over and knocked on the door to Mrs. Mercer's private rooms on the left side of the desk.

A few seconds after his knock, Mrs. Mercer opened the door and came out. "Sorry," she said cheerfully to the woman in the green dress. "Didn't hear you come in."

Mrs. Mercer looked at Ben and said gratefully, "Thanks, Ben."

The woman nodded to Ben formally and said, "Thank you."

"My pleasure," he said.

"What can I do for you," Mrs. Mercer said to the woman, drawing her attention away from Ben. As the woman and Mrs. Mercer walked toward the desk, Ben put on his hat and walked outside.

Chapter Twelve

The sun was getting hotter every day.

Ben was glad to have his hat to shut out the glaring midday sun, and realized how hungry he was.

He needed to go to the Horned Jackrabbit restaurant down the street, on the same side of the street as Mercer's. A horned jackrabbit was a cowboy's joking name for a longhorn cow, known both for its long horns and how fast it could go through the brush.

First, though, he walked up the street past the Assay office, the Gold Digger's Saloon, and Magee's livery stable. As he peered inside, he saw that Jimmy was no longer sitting on his chair inside the door reading. The chair was empty.

Right next to the livery stable was the tiny telegraph office run by Jeb Skeggs. It was Jeb Skeggs who had spoken up for him to Judge Colby. Jeb was the man that Ben had gotten the lumber for, after Jeb's house had burned. Luckily, Ben had a friend who ran a lumber mill. Technically, it was more to the northeast, but Jeb always called it to the north when he was telling the story, and Ben didn't correct him.

"Ben!" Jeb said, when he saw Ben walking by, and beckoned him in. Ben entered the front door of the small plank building.

"Glad to see you. Want you to know I think you got a raw deal," Jeb said, pumping Ben's hand up and down across the small counter that separated them.

He knew Jeb was dying to ask Ben where he had been but was too polite.

"Thanks," Ben said.

"Sheriff just had me send a message to Tucson," Jeb said. "Can't believe you found the Lost Prospector! Need my help with anything?"

"I guess not; not now, anyway," Ben said. What else was there to say? He didn't know what to say about getting back the ranch. He didn't even have a clue about what it was he was planning to do. Except watch, like the *mestizo* said to do.

"Friends here in town want to help out."

"Thanks," Ben said.

"Miguel still in Greenwater, Texas?"

"Yep. Might come back here, though. I hope soon," Ben said.

Ben's stomach rumbled.

"What in tarnation was that?" Jeb said, jokingly. "Thought I heard a explosion or mebbe a earthquake."

"Guess I better go visit the Horned Jackrabbit eating establishment mighty soon," Ben said.

"Guess you better," Jeb said, smiling. As Ben turned to leave, he saw that Jeb went to sit at the table behind him near the front window.

As he closed the door to the telegraph office, he felt a sudden jab of pain in his back, where the wound was. It was bearable, so he kept walking, thinking.

He walked back down the street until he was past Mercer's and the Assay office, and kept on going until he reached the Horned Jackrabbit restaurant. Just the short walk had made him sweat. He took out his handkerchief, removed his hat, and wiped off his forehead.

He left his hat off as he entered the restaurant. It was crowded but he found an empty table next to the front window, near the blue-and-white-checked curtains that blocked out the sun somewhat by going halfway up the windows. He hung his hat on a peg on the wall near the table. The table was empty near the windows because of the heat.

The restaurant was the kind of informal place that customers moved the chairs around themselves to suit how many people were sitting at the same table. There was one chair left at the one empty table.

He had the feeling that a few people—strangers— were looking at him oddly as he passed by the tables in the restaurant, but he figured that local gossip about him had spread even to newcomers in town. Or maybe they had already heard about him finding the Lost Prospector. He was surprised to think that he, of all people, was the subject of so much town excitement and gossip.

He sat down and looked around. He was surprised

to see that the same lady he had met in the hotel with the green dress was already here, busy, intently talking to the owner of the Horned Jackrabbit, Buckshot Fenton. She sure hadn't spent much time in her hotel room. Buckshot was the man who had told the story about Ben's helping out with his rebellious teenage son.

Buckshot took time out from talking to the lady to wave to Ben. Then he resumed talking to the lady. The lady was nodding, yes, to whatever Buckshot was saying. When the discussion was over, Buckshot walked over to the wall and picked off a blue-and-white-checkered apron that was hanging there on a peg. The material matched the window curtains. Buckshot handed the apron to the woman. She looked at the blue and white checks, and then at her green calico dress.

Ben smiled as if he could tell what she was thinking. From a woman's point of view, the dress wouldn't "go" with the apron. He had heard his mother say things like that when he was growing up. She did look a mite colorful as she tied the apron's strings behind her into a neat bow.

Even though the woman's dress was somewhat old and worn out, she obviously still cared about how she looked. Now that he looked, he saw that the dress was very clean, and had somehow managed to be ironed. He guessed that she had come in earlier on the stage.

She walked across the restaurant straight to his table, and stood directly beside him, closer than most women stood to a man. In fact, the material from her dress touched his trouser leg.

"We meet again, so soon?" she said, smiling cheerfully at him. Her smile was a real, nice, wide, genuine smile. It made his heart begin to thump. He was very aware of how close she stood. She smelled nice, like lavender or something.

"That man—Buckshot, I think his name is—my new boss—says to wait on you first—right away. He says you're an awful nice guy who's had some bad luck." She smiled again, and her eyes lit up with the smile.

"Nice to see you again," Ben said, smiling back up at her.

"What'll it be?" she said. "To eat, I mean," she added.

"A big slab of steak, fried potatoes, biscuits, applesauce, and about a gallon of coffee," Ben said.

"Got it," she said, and then as he turned back toward the table she came back, concerned.

"Did you know that there is blood on the back of your shirt?"

Dang! His back must have started bleeding when he pulled his muscles either getting down from Paddy or when he closed the telegraph office door. Now he understood why everyone had looked at him oddly as he walked to his seat.

"You ought to get the doctor to look at that," the woman said. "I assume that there's a doctor in Websterville," she added. "At least I hope there is."

"There is. At least, there was, last time I was here," Ben said.

"Well, you want to eat first, or shall I hold the food until you get back from the doctor's?"

"No. Eat first, doctor later. That's my plan."

"If you say so," she said reluctantly. "What happened to you? If you don't mind my asking," she said. "By the way, my name is Virginia."

"Ben Mitchell. Fell off my horse into some brush."

She made a face that told him that she didn't believe that for a minute, so he chuckled at her to let her know that he understood that she knew he was lying.

She left, and in a minute she was back with a plate of warm biscuits, a bowl of applesauce, and a big cup of coffee. She had managed to carry it all at once, by balancing the biscuits on the upper part of her bent arm, and cradling the bowl of applesauce with a bent wrist. She had the coffee in her other hand, holding the mug by the handle.

"Never was a very good liar," he said. She put the coffee down first, then began unloading the applesauce and biscuits off her other arm.

"With an open face like yours, I wouldn't suggest you try it that much. Lying, that is. You have an honest face, and you had a funny look on your face when you lied. I think I could catch you in a lie every time you did it," she said. "Steak and 'taters will take a few more minutes."

She left to wait on someone else.

When she came back a few minutes later with the

steak and potatoes, she put them down without speaking, and went and got him some more coffee.

As she poured the coffee he said, "You didn't take long to get a job and start working. Did you just arrive on the stage this morning?"

"I been takin' care of myself a while. Been cookin', cleanin', and waitin' on people since my father—the last of my family—died."

"I'm sorry." Ben thought to himself that he was grateful to have heard her story, especially right now. It reminded him that his own problems were small compared to what other people had.

"Don't be sorry. I'm fine," she said, proudly.

She left, and Ben remembered the look on her face that he had noticed earlier. The expression she had on her face before she had smiled, and her face lit up. It was one of tiredness. He was not the only one who had an "open face" that showed expression, how he was feeling. She did too.

Briefly, he wondered what *her* face would look like when she lied. If she lied. She was so blunt, maybe she didn't.

Now that he'd looked at her face more closely, he saw that she was really beyond just pretty. Verging on beautiful, although that was not a word he used often.

And well, anyone would look tired if they had just had a long, bumpy, stagecoach ride. He wondered where she had come from. How far she had ridden on the stagecoach. She didn't have a southern accent.

She disappeared into the back room. Ben suspected she was back there washing dishes.

He left without seeing her again. He paid another waitress for his meal, grabbed his hat, and left.

Buckshot Fenton waved to him as he left, even though he was busy with customers. "Talk to you later, Ben," Buckshot called to him from across the room as Ben got up to leave. Some of his anger at the town had cooled since his return; people, like Buckshot, had been trying to show him their loyalty and support. If he hadn't come back, he would never have known how loyal the people in this town were to him.

From the restaurant, Ben walked diagonally across the street two doors down from the Long Horn Saloon to the doctor's office. It was past the blacksmith's shop and Cavanaugh's General Store.

The doctor kept his office right in his house. A small, inconspicuous sign hung above the white painted door which stated in gold letters: Doctor Burns, Physician.

He'd been to the doctor's only once before, when he was covered with bee stings. Herding cattle, Ben had accidentally disturbed a nest. The bee stings hurt like heck, and the doctor had removed some stingers, then given him some salve to rub on the stings. Some of the stings had hurt off and on for a few days. Ollie and Ben had gone back at night when the bees were asleep in the nest and burned the hive.

He knocked at the door, and Doc Burns let him in. He was a tall, thin man, about forty-five or fifty years old with gray hair. He wore his round gold-framed eyeglasses down toward the tip of his nose, and looked at people over the top of them. Today, he had on a new gray suit.

Ben turned slightly so that the doctor could see his back.

"Let me see that," the doctor said, with his slight Scottish burr.

"Sit on the table there," he directed, as he walked with Ben to the table in the center of the room.

Ben sat.

"Take off your shirt."

Ben unbuttoned and took off his shirt, and Doctor Burns removed the dressing and examined the wound.

"Whoever took care of this gunshot wound did a good job," the doctor said.

Well, that ended that, Ben thought to himself. No sense trying to lie. The doctor already recognized the wound as a gunshot.

"You were lucky that that bullet only grazed your skin. An inch or two further in and you would be dead, or maybe even paralyzed, if it had hit your spine. Consider yourself darn lucky."

Ben chuckled inwardly at the doctor's mention of luck. Ben had pledged to himself not to believe in luck anymore. And now, ironically, the doctor was saying that he had had good luck.

Life has ways of almost laughing at you, Ben thought. Just when you think you've got something figured out. But the *mestizo* still had a point. If Ben hadn't been fond of Paddy and leaned forward to pat him to say "Thank you," he might be dead or paralyzed.

Was that luck, or not? Ben had to admit he didn't know.

The doctor washed the wound with soap. It stung like a son-of-a-gun when he did it. Then he put a clean dressing on the wound.

He scolded Ben as he worked. "If you hadn't opened this back up, it would have healed faster. What did you do to open this wound back up?"

"I'm not sure. I felt it hurt some when I was riding, and then when I closed a door, I could feel it wrench."

"Well, stay off your horse for a few days and close doors slowly and carefully for a few days too. I don't want this opening up again," the doctor said with a sarcastic smirk. Then he shrugged. "It's not deep. Just missed your spine. It should scab over in a couple of days. Try not to do anything else to make a worse problem out of this, like get it dirty.

"And come back in a few days and let me take a look at it and change the dressing. And get a new shirt, for God's sake, or at least wash this one," he scolded. "There's blood all over the back."

"I'll go next door to Cavanaugh's store right now," Ben said.

"You want to wait here and I'll have my wife go and get one for you? So that you don't have to put that bloody shirt on again over your clean bandage?"

The doctor didn't wait for an answer but walked rapidly to the back of the room and went through the door into the back of the house.

He came back a few seconds later with Mrs. Burns, who also spoke with a faint Scottish accent.

She was a bosomy lady with a jolly face and full rosy cheeks. She was close to the doctor's age, and wore her straight black hair neatly pulled back in a bun. She had on a dress covered with a pattern of small pink roses, with lace trim around the collar and cuffs.

Ben chuckled as he guessed that it was decided. The asking of the question was just a formality. Ben had no say in whether he was going or staying; Mrs. Burns was on her way.

Ben reached into his trousers to pull out some money to give Mrs. Burns, but she and Doctor Burns waved it away. "Pssht! Get out of here—you and your money—do you think we'd be takin' money from a decent man such as yerself that's been wronged so badly by that old bitter raccoon of a judge?" Mrs. Burns said angrily.

Ben knew that her anger was not at all directed at him but at the "old raccoon". He was very touched by both of the Burns's loyalty to him.

He sat, discussing the weather and other things with the doctor, until Mrs. Burns reappeared. She handed him a new medium blue shirt, and picked up the bloody light brown one.

"Come around to the back door tomorrow afternoon, around two o'clock, and I'll have this shirt clean and dry for you," she said. She smiled at him and opened the door at the back of the room leading to her and the doctor's private quarters.

With her hand on the doorknob she paused. "There might be a cup of tay fer you as well as a scone," she said, jokingly, "if you play your carrrds right, and say please."

"I'll be sure to do that," Ben said, smiling at her as she closed the door.

The doctor waved his hands away when Ben tried to pay him. "Get out of here," he said in a fond voice, "and mind my instructions."

Chapter Thirteen

Back out on the street, Ben didn't know what to do next.

He was tired. It had been a long day, and still he felt that he hadn't accomplished one thing toward the goal of getting at least his half of the ranch back.

He thought and worried as he went back up the street to Mercer's Hotel. He wished he had the money to offer to buy Lucy and David Woolsey out. The truth was, he didn't. Every penny he and Ollie had earned on the ranch they had put back into buying more horses for breeding and improving the ranch. All but necessary living expenses had gone right back into the ranch.

If Lucy hadn't gotten the ranch away from him, he might have been able to sell his half of the horses and pay her, or gotten a loan from the bank. That plan was nothing but a bitter joke now. Her new father-in-law owned the bank.

What could he do?

He tried to remember the advice the *mestizo* had given him. What did the old man say to do? What was it, exactly, the old man had said? Something like "The Apache side of me says you should go back and study."

But study what?

"Learn the weaknesses of David and Lucy and even David's father." Ben remembered him saying that.

But what weaknesses did they have?

None that he knew of.

Then what did he say to do?

"You must ask yourself," the old *mestizo* had said, "why did David's father do this? Find out what lie Lucy told to get this man to believe that he should lie and say that he was a witness to something that never happened."

Those might not be the exact words, but it was something close to that.

"Study them all. Look for their weaknesses, and you may get your ranch back."

And last, the old man said that if he used his *brains,* he would not need luck.

But what?

How?

What could he do?

He reached the hotel and went back in. Mrs. Mercer was there, and he asked her to send up some hot water so that he could wash. He would have liked to take a bath, but he was afraid of getting the new bandage wet. He would have to just wash all over as best he could.

She said, "The water will be up in a few minutes," and handed him some soap, a washcloth, and a towel from one of the shelves underneath the counter.

"Thanks," he said, as he took them from her.

Back upstairs in his room, he tried to puzzle out what he should do next. Use your brains.

He sat on the bed, then lay back, and had almost dozed off when he heard a quiet knock on the door.

"Who is it?" he asked.

"Water man," the voice said.

Ben walked over and opened the door. He was a bit taken aback to see it was Brady, Buckshot's teenage son. He had gotten older looking, and taller since the last time Ben had seen him a few months ago.

"You the hot water man in Mercer's Hotel now?" Ben asked.

"Sure looks like that, don't it?" Brady said teasingly. Ben knew that Brady was named for Mathew Brady, the well-known Civil War photographer. Mathew Brady, who was of Irish descent, had been born in Warren County, New York, where Buckshot's family was also originally from, Ben knew.

One day over lunch, on a slow day, Buckshot had told him all about his family's connection to Mathew Brady. He thought that he might be distantly related to the famous photographer. Ben couldn't remember all the details. Buckshot said that he didn't know for sure that it was true, but he had been told that ever since he was a child, and he believed it.

At any rate, Ben was glad to see that young Brady Fenton was working at a regular job now, and he said that.

Brady, who was medium height—so far—like his father, took after his mother in everything else. Especially personality. He had his mother's yellow hair and a pleasant face. Where Buckskin was big-boned and had a round belly, his son had a slim figure and was small-boned.

Brady walked further into the room and put the wooden bucket of hot water on the floor next to the table near the window. Then he came over to Ben.

"Feel these muscles, Ben," he said proudly, flexing his arm and putting out his jutting elbow toward Ben. "Hard as a rock from carrying buckets of water all the time."

Ben felt the boy's upper arm. Sure enough, there was a muscle the size of a small, round, hard egg there. Ben made a face to show he was impressed, and shook his head in approval. It was good to see the kid working and not getting into any trouble.

"I'm proud of you. Shows you're a hard worker."

He thought about saying "just like your father", but in this case, he felt he better not say it. Brady was at the stage where he didn't *want* to be like his father. Instead, Ben fished around in his pocket and gave Brady a big tip. Brady *had* brought the water up fast.

"Thanks, Mr. Mitchell," Brady said, with a raise of his eyebrows in pleasure at the size of the tip.

"Let me know if you need anything else." Brady smiled awkwardly as he went out, closing the door behind him.

So far, Brady was practically the only person who hadn't mentioned the loss of the ranch to Ben.

Ben chuckled. It was difficult growing up, and trying to find your place somewhere in the grown-up world. It was not just the *mestizo* who had trouble. Maybe all young people did.

Carrying hot water in a hotel was not such a bad start. He thought that Brady might be a person who liked people, like Mrs. Mercer. He didn't appear to want to be a cowboy, or live on a ranch. Brady had been raised in town, living with his mother and father in the back rooms of the restaurant, which opened at six every morning.

Right now too, Brady didn't want to work for his father. He wanted to prove himself. Be different from his father. Working for Mrs. Mercer was a good choice, then, for the purpose of making it on his own, and proving to his father he could make it on his own terms.

Ben chuckled. He could see some similarity. He didn't want to go home to Greenwater, Texas with his tail between his legs, either. He didn't want to go back to his hometown feeling like a failure, having lost the ranch he and Ollie had worked so hard for.

Once again he felt the pain of losing Ollie.

He poured some water from the bucket into the pitcher on the table by the window. From the pitcher, he poured some water into the bowl. He closed the clean white curtains, undressed, and began to wash. It took a few minutes to wash his whole body with soap and water. He had to be careful not to bust open his wound, so he washed slowly and carefully. Halfway through he got tired and winded, and had to sit on the bed to finish.

As he gently scrubbed and rinsed, using water from the pitcher and bucket, he began to plan what it was he would do next.

Chapter Fourteen

If he was to study their weaknesses, he had to learn about them first.

What did he know about David? David seemed the weakest link. Certainly, he had fallen for Lucy's charms as quickly as Ollie.

He had seen David around town. Knew him enough to say "Howdy" to. Seen him in church. Seen him going in and out of the land office. He knew David spent a lot of his free time—before he was married, at least—in the Long Horn Saloon.

The Long Horn Saloon was the saloon that Ben, himself, didn't much care for. It was the one with all the bullet holes in the walls, ceiling, and floors. A rougher crowd hung out at the Long Horn than at the other saloons in town. Men who didn't mind trouble hung out there. Ben didn't want trouble. He just wanted his ranch back. Ben didn't like the atmosphere in there. But he guessed that for a while, he'd be spending more time there. Might as well start tonight.

He finished washing, got dressed, and lay down on the bed to rest. He might as well begin right away.

He fell asleep, and when he woke, it was dark. He got up and went downstairs, carrying his hat.

Mrs. Mercer must have heard him coming down the stairs, because she opened the door to her private living quarters and said, "I don't usually do this, but would you like to have a sandwich and coffee in here?"

Ben said, "Thanks."

He had never heard of Mrs. Mercer being anything but businesslike before with clients in her hotel. He followed her, and entered what was a nicely furnished living room. There was a cream-colored silk sofa with a curved back, and top trim made of dark shiny wood that was carved into elaborate scrolls. There was also a matching armchair of the same material and trim. She had modern-looking hanging oil lamps that swung out from the walls on hinges and were attached by ornate black wrought iron hangers.

The oil lamps on the table had large circular white globes with roses painted on them. A lamp sat at each end of the sofa on tables that matched the wood of the sofa trim.

Another matching table sat in front of the sofa. It appeared that Mrs. Mercer had a lot more money than he had realized.

Through a doorway on the left, he could see a very up-to-date modern kitchen. Two more doorways were on the right. He guessed one must be the door to her bedroom, and he didn't know what the other door was for. Could be to a storage cellar, or another bedroom. He had no idea.

Mrs. Mercer motioned that he should sit on the sofa. He did, awkwardly, worrying that his black trousers would dirty the fancy light-colored fabric. He laid his black hat beside him carefully. He would have been more comfortable if the sofa were dark brown or black, he joked inwardly to himself.

Mrs. Mercer hurried into the kitchen and returned with a tray. She must have had it ready for a while, because the sandwich was already made, and was on a plate with an upside-down bowl on top of it, evidently keeping the bread from drying out.

He took the bowl off. The sandwich was roast beef, piled high. The bread was thickly sliced and freshly made. Beside the plate was a mug of coffee, a spoon, and a sugar bowl.

"Do you take sugar in your coffee?"

"When I can get it," Ben said, grinning.

Mrs. Mercer's eyes twinkled. Ben knew she was a widow. Her hair was grayish-brown and she wore it pulled back above her ears, where it then fell in soft waves down past her neck. It was neatly parted in the middle.

She smiled, and then said, "I don't suppose you know—or maybe you do—that John Woolsey is my cousin."

"No, I didn't." Ben tried to hide his surprise.

"You've always been a decent young man, and I

. . . well, I just want to tell you this. John's wife has been to see me a few times since . . . your troubles, and she told me that ever since . . . what happened. . . . John hasn't been able to sleep nights. That's never happened before. I was wondering if you could tell me what, exactly, is going on."

Mrs. Mercer was a good person. Ben knew that as surely as he knew his own mother was a good person. It was a gut feeling about Mrs. Mercer's goodness that prompted him to tell her exactly what had happened—right from the beginning—that first day when Lucy had captured Ollie's heart, the day Lucy had gotten off the stage. He told her how the three of them had forged papers saying he had sold Ollie the ranch:

Mrs. Mercer was a good listener, and was silent until Ben finished. He finished his story at the point when he rode out of town.

He thought about the Lost Prospector.

"What is it?" Mrs. Mercer said. "I can see by your face that you've just thought of something else. What is it? Can you tell me about it?"

Ben told her about the Lost Prospector, Samuel Logan, and how he had found him.

"That was good of you to bury him, and make him a little cross," Mrs. Mercer said. "Eat. All this talking has stopped you from eating. I'm sorry."

"Don't be. It was good to tell someone," Ben said. He meant that. It was good to tell a woman, for a change.

He told her that he had brought the gun, holster,

and gold back to town and given it to Sheriff Squibb. He finished the sandwich and coffee.

"About the ranch, I believe you, Ben, I want to tell you that right off. So will John's wife. She has been married to him for too many years not to know when John's made a mistake. She's had to deal with the fact that John's made 'mistakes' before. In some ways, John's a weak man.

"If he lied to get what he thought was 'justice' for Lucy, if he thought that you had lied, it has been on his conscience ever since. Don't worry. I'll do what I can to make things right."

That was nice of her, but Ben doubted that she could do anything. "My lawyer says that the judge is reluctant to admit he made a bad decision. He won't overturn his decision. Doesn't want to lose face, admit he made a mistake," Ben told her.

She made a face of disapproval. "Judge Colby is a tough, hard man. I don't like him much. Never have. Respect him even less."

"I guess I can echo that feeling," Ben said.

He didn't want to let on to Mrs. Mercer that he planned to do some detective work in the Long Horn Saloon. He didn't want to lie to her either, so he said, which was the truth, "I need to go and check on my horse."

Mrs. Mercer said, "Of course. I didn't mean to keep you."

They both got up, and Ben understood why Mrs. Mercer could hear when people came down. The stairs came down in an area so that she could hear boots on the stairway from either her bedroom or her living room. Though probably not when she was in her kitchen.

Boots made a rather loud noise as men went up and down the stairs, but he heard one set of softer, lighter footsteps that sounded like a woman. He wondered if it was the new girl coming home from her first long day of work at the Horned Jackrabbit.

The restaurant closed at dusk every evening, but the help had to stay later to clean up and get everything ready for the next day. They had to do things like put beans to soak overnight and pre-fry bacon for the earliest customers.

Mrs. Mercer picked up the tray, brought it into the kitchen, and then returned and walked him to the door.

"See you tomorrow," she said.

"Thanks, Mrs. Mercer."

Chapter Fifteen

He walked through the lobby and outside. It was a clear starry night, one of those nights when you could see so far it almost made you dizzy to look too long up at the stars.

He walked to the livery stable, and checked on Paddy. Paddy turned to nuzzle him affectionately.

"I miss you too," Ben said to the horse, patting him on the neck and rubbing Paddy's chest. He felt foolish saying that to the horse, but it was true. Paddy had been his one constant companion for a while now.

He stayed a few minutes. Paddy seemed to be fine. The stall was clean, and so was Paddy. James Magee had curried him.

There was a gray-and-white-striped tomcat that lived in the stable. Ben had seen the cat before. Now it was looking toward Ben. The cat seemed very impatient with Ben's presence there. Ben chuckled at how clearly the old tomcat was indicating that it was annoyed: putting back his ears and making a disgruntled face as he crouched, moving very slowly, stalking with almost imperceptible movements at the edge of a stall near the back used to store grain. He was clearly waiting for Ben to leave.

The cat was probably hunting the rats that came to steal the grain in the stable, Ben thought. Ben's presence was obviously interfering with the cat's work, and he wasn't happy about it. "All right, all right, I'm going," Ben said to the cat.

Chuckling, Ben left the livery stable and walked to the Long Horn Saloon. He took a deep breath, pulled his hat down as far over his face as he could, and went inside. It smelled of spilled beer and whiskey, and was dimly lit by oil lamps, all except a table near the back where men were playing cards. That area, near the left back wall, was the table closest to the bar, and was well lit.

He walked to the bar, ordered a whiskey, and returned to a chair close to the bar, opposite the card table, with his back to the wall. He didn't recognize anyone in the bar. With a start, he realized that it was Friday night. That's why it was so crowded.

He sat far down in the chair and kept his hat down over his eyes. Although he took small sips from his glass now and then, he tried to give the impression that he was dozing, and not listening.

But he was.

He was there about fifteen minutes when he saw David Woolsey come in. He had talked to himself—

he hoped not out loud—and prepared himself not to move a muscle if he saw David enter. He thought he had succeeded, as David didn't even glance his way before rudely telling a small man to get out of a seat at the monte table and let David have his seat.

The man did. Immediately. Either David's status had gone up, or his reputation in this bar was different—tougher—than the one Ben was familiar with in town.

Was David a bully?

His own impression of David Woolsey had been that he was close to his father, a churchgoer—not a gunman, in any sense of the word. Yet the man at the table had given up his seat without an argument, as if he were scared of him or his power. Usually, in the Long Horn Saloon, that meant skill with a Colt .45.

Maybe the small man was just holding the seat for David. Somehow, from the frightened look on the man's face Ben doubted that that had been it.

Was this the first fact he had discovered, in his work as Detective Mitchell? Ben joked to himself. *Was David a bully? And did he like to have power over people?*

Ben listened for about a half hour more. If he wanted to stay longer, he would need to buy another drink. With the wound on his back draining his energy, another drink and he would be under the table sleeping—and maybe talking out loud again.

Great detecting that would be.

Luckily, David's back was toward Ben, so he picked up his empty glass, brought it over, put it on the bar, and said a quiet good-night to the bartender. He was safe doing that because he didn't recognize the bartender. He was new since Ben had been in the Long Horn Saloon.

As he walked by the monte table, no one turned and looked. In fact, no one paid the least bit of attention to him, and he walked back outside. It was time to turn in for the night.

Tomorrow he was having "tay"—tea—with Mrs. Burns (going to try to do a little more detective work), and see if Mrs. Mercer had come up with anything about John Woolsey.

He went back to the hotel. He said "Good Evenin' " to Mrs. Mercer who was sitting in a chair by the front window with a small gray kitten in her lap. She was busy petting the cat, so Ben went upstairs. He was glad that he didn't have to talk to her anymore right now. He was tired and wanted to go to sleep.

In the morning, he asked Brady for hot water, and washed and shaved, then walked to the Horned Jack-rabbit and ate breakfast. It was crowded because it was Saturday. Another waitress waited on him, and he didn't get a chance to talk to Virginia or Buckshot. They were both very busy.

After breakfast, he headed across the street to Jim Cavanaugh's store. He poked around as if he was looking for something, but he was really listening to see if the women who came in mentioned any of the three Woolseys. Maybe because he was there, they didn't.

Finally, he bought a bar of soap, a pair of white

socks, and some writing paper and envelopes. The one bar of soap in his saddlebags had gotten a lot of use in his trip to the canyon, and had gotten smaller and smaller until it was nothing but a flat white sliver. He needed the paper and envelopes to write to Miguel.

After that, he walked back across the street and past the restaurant back to Mercer's, went upstairs, and dropped off the paper and the soap on the table in his room. He took off his old socks with the hole in one of them and threw them away. Then he put on his new socks and put his boots back on.

He left his room and went back outside, walking up the street past the Assay office, the Gold Digger's Saloon, and then into the open doorway of James Magee's livery.

Jimmy was currying one of two new horses that had just come in. One was a sorrel and the other a small black mustang.

"Mornin' Ben," Jimmy said. "You here to fetch Paddy?"

"No. Not quite yet," Ben said.

"That's good," Jimmy said. "Paddy could use some grain for a few more days. That, and some rest. You both been on a long trip, it seems."

"We were." Paddy had been great. Jimmy was right, the dependable horse could use a rest, and needed to put some weight back on.

"Go north, did ya?"

"Yes."

Was Jimmy questioning him? This was unlike

Jimmy, who, as the livery man, knew, better than anyone, the danger of asking too many questions.

Ben sensed that Jimmy was trying to be friendly and make conversation, but the usual thing would have been to discuss the weather, things other than where it was Ben had gone.

He decided that in this case, honesty—or maybe bluntness—was called for. With a smile he said, "Jim, what's this all about?"

He could tell that Jim was worried. He stopped currying the withers of the sorrel he was working on, and motioned Ben to come into a crude room that had been made out of one of the front stalls. Harnesses and other stored equipment were hanging from pegs on the walls, and were stuffed on shelves.

"Fact is, last night, late, John Woolsey came banging on my door." His face showed distaste, and some worry. His brow showed all worry lines as he said, "Dag blasted Woolsey. His bank has a mortgage on my livery stable. Fact is, the man's always been decent enough, up to now.

"But he was lookin' worried. Saw you were back in town. Must of figgered that you'd leave your horse here, like you did when you were stayin' at Mercer's before."

Jimmy rubbed his chin nervously, scratching the stubble from not shaving this morning. He reached over and put the curry comb on one of the shelves, then nervously stuffed his hands into his pants pockets. He bent his elbows, then leaned up against the doorway.

"He didn't outright threaten me, but he insinuated that I might be a big help to him if I kept an eye on you. I have no intention of doin' that to a friend. I wanted to know where you went for my own information to try and figger out what was goin' on. What in tarnation *is* goin' on? Are you back here to try and get your land back? I'm on your side, but I want you to know that it might be foolhardy, stirrin' up trouble. You got three or four pretty powerful people on the other side, against you. The judge, for one, and John and David Woolsey. I don't want you to get hurt."

"Why is the judge against me? I know why the Woolseys are—they managed to steal my half of the ranch," Ben said.

"Pure stubbornness, is what I hear. Pigheadedness; that's Judge Colby. And I think that John made up his mind you did it—sold your ranch to Ollie. He thought that he was just helping her get what was legally hers. That's what I think, anyways. But I never believed that part about you destroying the papers that proved you'd sold your half to Ollie."

Jimmy didn't say that he didn't believe that Ben sold the land to Ollie. Ben felt that he had to set Jimmy straight. And he had to get Jimmy to believe him.

"Jimmy, I don't know what you've been told. I know some people still believe that I sold my half of the ranch to Ollie. The truth was, Ollie didn't want me to leave. He asked me not to, and persuaded me to stay on for a couple of years. Said he needed me. And the truth was, after he died, I was stupid. Didn't think to go in and mess with the paperwork about the ranch. Left it all where it was—where Lucy could get at it. One of them, I think it was Lucy, to tell the truth, forged my name to a bill of sale.

"It's been hard to get people to believe me. But I never sold my half of the ranch." Ben said the last sentence forcefully, looking Jimmy right in the eyes, hoping that Jimmy would believe him.

Jimmy had been looking sharply at Ben the whole time Ben was talking, as if assessing whether he thought Ben was lying. He had removed his hands from his pockets and crossed them over his chest as if to say, "Prove it" when Ben had begun talking, but as Ben finished, Jimmy stood up straight, no longer leaning back against the wooden doorway in a cynical gesture.

"I wouldn't say stupid. You were grieving over the loss of your only brother." Jimmy looked for a moment as if he were going to pat Ben on the shoulder, but he didn't.

"And it looks like while you were grieving, Lucy wasn't. She was too busy makin' plans fer her own future. I woulda probably left the papers in her bedroom too. Woulda felt funny goin' into my brother's wife's bedroom lookin' fer things after he died an' all."

With relief, Jimmy took a step as if he were going to leave the small room, and then he stopped.

"All right. Whatever you do, do me one favor. I'm in a tight spot. Do what you are going to, but do it out of my sight. I got one more payment to make to

John Woolsey. Supposed to make it the end of next week. If I don't know what you're doing, I can't tell Woolsey, can I? After I make the payment, I'm on your side. Until then, keep me in the dark. After that, anything I can do to help. . . ."

"Thanks, Jimmy, for the straight talk."

"No tellin' who else in town John Woolsey is pullin' this—well, I call it almost a blackmail stunt—on. So watch your back."

"Thanks."

Well, Ben thought. *So much for expecting help from John Woolsey.*

Jimmy took a step and picked up a bucket of grain, and the two men walked back to where the two horses were waiting.

As Jimmy went back to work, Ben walked out into the bright Arizona sunlight. Another scorcher.

Chapter Sixteen

The truth was, he missed home. The ranch. The valley where the ranch was, was beautiful. You could get out of the midday sun by walking along the creek under the trees. The horses often did that very thing.

He did his best to hang around town, listening, for a couple of hours, but he didn't learn anything helpful.

It was close to two o'clock, so Ben decided that he'd stop in for his cup of "tay" at Mrs. Burns's house.

For that, he had to walk halfway back down through town. The doctor's house was down at the south end of town.

He walked down the same side of the street until he got to the Horned Jackrabbit, then across the street to the doctor's house. As he crossed, he had to dodge a wagon with a woman driving and five children in the back. They were pulling up in front of Cavanaugh's, and the children in the wagon bed were excitedly talking about candy. They had evidently been promised some.

He reached the Burnses' house. She'd said to come around to the back door, so he did. The back of the house was as fancy as the front, because it served as the entrance to the Burnses' living quarters.

The back door had a fancy door knocker made of brass. The part you lifted up to knock was the brass "handle" of a basket of flowers. The part that the knocker hit was the basket of flowers, also made of brass. He'd never seen one like it; he wondered if it had come with them from Scotland.

He used the knocker. Mrs. Burns opened the door within a few seconds. "Come in, young man," she said in her friendly way. He saw that his shirt, all clean and ironed neatly, was hung over one of the dining room chairs.

He stepped into the hallway. There were two rooms that he could see. To the left was a dining room, with a table with a white lace tablecloth on it and six chairs made of dark, shiny highly polished wood.

To the right was a small living room, also nicely decorated. Although the end tables were plain, the curtains on the living room windows were of heavy gold brocade, with gold fringe, and tied back with tassels. The curtains didn't look new, but as if they had belonged to the Burnses for a few years.

The two rooms were connected by a large arched doorway.

Mrs. Burns took him into the living room, where the sofa was shiny brown brocade with gold tassels that matched those on the curtains. Her oil lamps were large and also had flowers on the glass globe sections, but the flowers were not roses like the ones on Mrs. Mercer's oil lamps, but some other smaller flowers, mostly whites and browns.

On the table in front of the couch was a neat tray with two teacups and a plate full of scones and cookies. The scones were large and the cookies dainty and small. The cookies looked like either molasses or gingerbread.

He sat down and she poured a cup of tea from the teapot into one of the two dainty white cups. The cups and saucers had tiny pink flowers and gold trim around the edges. The cup was small and he was afraid that he would drop it or break it.

As he took it, he realized that the handle was so small, he would have a hard time slipping his finger through the handle, so he didn't. He held it by grasping the handle between his fingers.

Mrs. Burns noticed and chuckled. "Sorry," she said. "The doctor's fingers are small, and I guess that these cups are a bit out of place in a cowboy's hands. These are my mother's cups. They were her pride and joy: pure bone china. From the old country."

"They've come a long way," Ben said. "Must have been difficult getting them here without breaking."

"That it was," Mrs. Burns said. "That it was," she continued in her Scottish accent. "We packed the dishes in barrels of flour for the sea voyage."

She held out the plate of scones and cookies.

"Here, have a scone or some cookies."

Ben took a scone. He bit into it and was surprised that it was so delicious. It looked similar to a biscuit, but the flavor was totally different. He realized, after a minute, that it had chopped up pecans in it, such as he had had back in Texas, as well as some other flavoring he was unfamiliar with. Even the texture was different from a regular biscuit.

"This is delicious," he said. "Did you learn to make these in Scotland?"

"Aye," she said, pleased.

He wondered if she, like other people in town, had had him there for a reason, other than giving him his shirt back.

As they talked, he gathered that she didn't. She was just trying to be friendly. Evidently, she was sorry that the land had been taken from him unjustly. He gathered from what she said that back in the old country, land had been taken that way at times, and so she felt bad about it happening here too.

Mostly, she seemed glad just to talk to him about Scotland. She missed Scotland, just as much as he missed his horse ranch. They had a lot in common.

She told a story about how back in Scotland, a neighbor—a mean, stingy man—had gained a reputation for beating his Shetland ponies. The men of the community had gathered together, gone to the man's croft, and horsewhipped him.

They told him that if they ever heard of him beating another pony, they would be back and do worse to him. As far as she knew, he never beat any of his ponies again. He knew the men of the small village would keep their word and come back if they caught him at it again.

"The men used ponies to carry peat back from the moors to the crofts," she explained. "Crofts are like what you would call a small farm here. Some of them were rental properties."

"Men back in Texas near my father's ranch did the same thing to one of our distant neighbors. He beat his horses, and a bunch of men, well . . . did about the same thing."

In fact, most people had considered the man lucky that he didn't get strung up. Especially one neighbor who had sold valuable horses to the man. He had been horrified to find the horses that he had raised from colts starving, and with scarred backs from repeated beatings.

All the man's horses had been ruined by his bad treatment of them.

"Luckily, bad treatment of horseflesh is rare," Ben said.

"And a good thing it is," Mrs. Burns added.

"Have a cookie," she urged, as he finished his tea. She poured him another cup, taking the teapot in one hand and lifting the white cup to the spout of the teapot with the other.

She joked, "I think you're getting the hang of hanging onto the wee little cup," as he reached out to take the tiny handle again.

"Maybe I am," he said, laughing. He ate one of the cookies. It was molasses, as he had guessed. It was very good. He ate another scone. He left shortly after that, thanking Mrs. Burns for her hospitality as he left.

He walked around to the front of the house and back across the street.

He didn't know what to do next. He was free until this evening. He was planning to go back to the Long Horn and listen and watch again. As he walked up the street, he thought of the Gold Digger's Saloon up next to the livery stable. It was after three o'clock. Maybe he'd take a look in there. It was the saloon that he and Ollie had liked the best in town, although he'd rarely had the time or the money to go in there. In the Gold Digger's Saloon, he might see people that he knew.

He headed up the street. As he passed the Horned Jackrabbit, he met Mrs. Mercer coming out. She had a parasol to keep the sun off, and she opened it as she walked alongside him.

"Left Brady at the desk. I had cabin fever," she joked. "Had to get out of that place for a few minutes. Came to the Jackrabbit for coffee. That nice Virginia Jackson works there. Came into the town on the stage from Tucson, you know."

Her last name was Jackson, then. And she had come from Tucson.

"I asked her if she knew Lucille back in Tucson."

It took a moment for him to understand. Lucille— Lucy. Maybe she knew Lucy back in Tucson!

"What did she say about her?"

"Not much. Nothing, really, just that she never heard of her. Lots of people in Tucson now. Virginia was busy. Didn't have time to talk much. Not one to gossip."

They had reached the hotel, and Mrs. Mercer took ahold of the doorknob to open it. She paused. "I haven't given up yet, on trying to help you with your problem."

"Thanks, Mrs. Mercer." he said, smiling.

"No problem, Mr. Mitchell," she said, and then turned the doorknob and went inside.

Because she hadn't mentioned her cousin—John Woolsey—Ben knew that the talk with John hadn't gone well. That didn't surprise him after talking to Jimmy Magee at the livery stable. He felt that her silence on the subject was somewhat an apology for not being able to help him yet with his problem with John.

He walked on up to the Gold Digger's Saloon. Inside, there was the usual amount of people for an afternoon. Many more men would be in later. There were about a dozen men already there. The place smelled of spilled beer and whiskey, and smoke from cigarettes and cigars.

In this saloon, there was the usual mix of fifty percent miners, forty percent cowboys, and ten percent other occupations.

Shorty Squibb was at a table surrounded by half a dozen men, some sitting and some standing around. Ben recognized some of the men. He knew most of them well enough to nod to when he saw them around town.

They were all drinking whiskey, except for Shorty, who had a cup of coffee in front of him. No one ap-

peared to be drunk. Shorty acknowledged Ben's presence, which immediately included him into the group,
and then continued his conversation. It appeared to be
about the judge.

"He's like a sheriff I knew back in New Mexico
Territory," Shorty said. "Once that dag blasted man
made up his mind someone was guilty, even if the real
shooter was standin' there with his pistol barrel so hot
you'd burn yer fingers if you touched it, and with blisters from shootin' on his trigger finger, that sheriff
would twist things around so that he'd accuse the innocent man that he'd already laid hold of.

"He'd say the one he blamed for the killings had
shoved the hot gun into the other man's hand so hard
that that was why that man's trigger finger had blisters.
That was the way he was. There was no changing the
sheriff's mind. That was why I left there an' come
here. Here, at least up 'til now. . . ."

He trailed off from talking. He motioned to Ben.

"Here, sit a spell. Was yer ears burnin? We was
talkin' about Judge Colby. Claim jumper knocked Al
Guerney here on the head on the way to town to register his claim, and the judge backs the claim jumper
up."

Ben looked, and noticed that one of the men had a
big goose egg on the side of his head. "You have Doc
Burns take a look at that?" Ben said, concerned.

Al Guernsey nodded his head gingerly, yes.

Another man said, "I took him to the doc. He said
it will be all right. Take a few days for the bump to
go down."

Al said, "It was a while before I came to and made it back to town. By then, the crook had come in, registered the claim as his own. I was out of luck."

"Anybody seen you workin' the claim?" Ben said. "Any witnesses?"

Al said, "No. That's just it. I had just discovered the dang thing myself. Looked like a good vein. Down toward the Vultures."

He meant the Vulture Mountains.

"Claim jumper was slick. Registered the claim, sold it, then disappeared—left town—and a crew of strangers come to begin digging," Shorty said. "I figger that the claim jumper had been watching Al for some time. That makes me worry some about other men out there alone, digging. Some of them have plumb disappeared.

"Al made it back alive; he was left for dead. Someone maybe be watching prospectors out there, wait 'til they find something, and then make sure they don't make it back to town. Might be even more than one. A gang. Judge Colby says 'hogwash.' But I got no reason to disbelieve Al, here."

"Or the lump on his head. Looks like the bushwhacker tried to crack Al's skull, good," one of the other miners said to Ben.

It sure looked that way. It was a nasty goose-egg-sized lump on Al's forehead, Ben thought.

"Judge been actin' weird lately," one of the cowboys said.

Shorty Squibb raised his eyebrows. "You're right, come to think of it. Colby was all right until lately. Thought it was because he was sick of judgin' and' gettin' on in years," he said, "but now that I think on it, I think you're right," he said to the cowboy. "He's gettin' weird, all right."

Shorty got up, pushing back his chair. "You gave me somethin' to chaw upon. I ain't sayin' right out Colby's crooked, I'm just sayin' he's made some odd decisions lately." He left, giving them all the impression that he was going back to his office down the street to think on it.

After he left the men talked further, and it was a fifty-fifty split whether or not the men thought that Colby was outright crooked, or just making bad decisions.

The cowboys tended to think that he was just making mistakes, but the miners felt strongly that he had turned crooked.

A few other well-known miners had mysteriously disappeared in the area surrounding town in the last few months, and that was why a bunch of miners had gone to Sheriff Squibb and put up a reward of three thousand dollars. That was where the new poster Ben had seen outside the Sheriff's office had originated.

Over the next few nights, Ben spent a lot of time in the Long Horn Saloon. He added some facts about David Woolsey to his collection. David was pompous, and a fool; he found that out right away. Some of these things he heard other men say when David wasn't there. Other things, he saw for himself. He saw the first real chink in David's armor on Wednesday night.

In the afternoon on Wednesday, Ben went and got

his dressing changed. Doctor Burns said that if he came in on the next Saturday, the dressings could be removed for good. And later that night, in the Long Horn, Ben sat unnoticed in his inconspicuous chair in the corner near the wall. If David had ever noticed him coming in to the Long Horn, he gave no indication.

Evidently, Ben was too "small potatoes" to be noticed or acknowledged. David had taken all he could get from Ben Mitchell and was through with him.

Ben gathered from teasing remarks being made to David by his companions at the monte table that the marriage wasn't going too well. Lucy spent most of her time at Cedar Creek Ranch, and it was obvious that David spent most of his evenings at the Long Horn.

From the joking and teasing, he gathered that the men in the saloon had the impression that Lucy didn't much care where David was. Lucy's new husband had evidently served his purpose and been discarded, for the most part. Which didn't appear to bother David, as he cozied up to the women who hung around the Long Horn.

When David entered the Long Horn on Wednesday night, the table of card players was an unusual bunch. The five men—strangers—had come in together late in the afternoon and, even for the Long Horn, were a rough-looking bunch.

Their guns were tied down, and David, taking a look at them, decided to forego the usual monte game and sat instead at a table near the front door, about six tables away from where Ben pretended to be dozing with his hat pulled down partially over his face, listening. Two or three cowboys and miners were at the table where David chose to sit, and the miners were bragging about their muscles. Using the picks and shovels day after day had produced good-sized muscles in their upper arms. The cowboys were also well muscled, Ben noticed, from roping and tying as well as doing other ranch chores.

The men in David's group rolled up their sleeves and began to arm wrestle on the table in the saloon. Right from the start, Ben saw that David was deadly serious in his quest to be the best. These contests were no joke to David Woolsey; he was very competitive. Again and again, he cheated as much as he could, beginning the match before the other man's elbow was set and ready.

David was the biggest man of the group, and Ben could see that he was used to winning. He had the advantage on most of the men, who were smaller than he was, with shorter arms. As a result, he won most of the matches, until they caught on to what he was doing. The whiskeys they had consumed since early afternoon made them a little slow to realize, at first, what he was doing.

After that, when David was made to wait until a count of three, he began to lose. He was a poor loser. He stormed out when he lost to a huge miner named Adolph Ritter.

But Ben had seen something in David's behavior. David could not seem to turn down a chance to show off; to prove that he was the best. How could Ben use that to his advantage? Was there any way to use this one defect—this one weakness—to get his ranch back?

It struck him that it would be ironic justice to use David, legally, to get the ranch back, just as Lucy had used David, illegally, to get the ranch in the first place. If only he could think of how. . . .

Chapter Seventeen

The first light of dawn woke him up, coming in through the window of his room in Mercer's Hotel. He slid to the side of the bed.

An idea occurred to him as reached down beside the bed for his boots. As he began to pull them on, he thought again about the gift of the *mestizo*.

Had the *mestizo* been thinking carefully about Ben's problem when he'd taken so long to choose a gift to give Ben? Ben didn't think the *mestizo* did anything randomly. He always thought things out carefully, it had seemed to Ben. Was the *mestizo* sending him a *message* by giving him the moccasins?

Has the mestizo sent me a clue as to what to do? How to solve my problem? Ben thought. *The moccasins. Of course.*

He began to have an idea of what it was that the gift of the moccasins was telling him to do.

But would it, could it work?

The success of it would depend on a few things. It would have to be planned well, and using every bit of advice the old man gave him.

He looked though the pile of things in the corner of the room that he had brought with him from the stable. The small bag made of rabbit fur was in the pile. He took the moccasins and laces out of the bag and brought them over to the side of the bed. Removing the boots, he put the moccasins on.

They fit. Beautiful creamy buckskin, they covered his legs all the way up to his knees. And the old man had included long, perfectly cut thin leather straps to tie them securely in a crisscross manner up his thighs. Good for traveling in areas with prickers and thorns. Maybe even tough for a snake to bite through.

He took them back off, and put his boots back on. At least now he had the beginnings of a plan. . . .

A little while later he was outside of town riding Paddy south, with the small rabbit fur bag hanging from the saddle. He had filled his canteens from a public well near the south end of town. As soon as he was far enough outside of town so that he was out of sight and could not be seen, he picketed Paddy and put the moccasins on again.

He ran a short distance, glad that it was early morning and the glare of the sun was not so bad, and that the area was not overly loaded with prickly pear cactuses. He ran some more. Although he was in good shape, with not an ounce of fat on him, he tired faster than he thought he would, and at a shorter distance. Perhaps it was the wound.

He realized that he needed practice. His heart was pounding and he was huffing and puffing as he made it back to where Paddy stood, looking quizzically. Ben laughed, then holding his sides because they hurt from running, he plopped down in the dirt to rest.

Paddy was probably thinking what the heck was I doing running, when Paddy was right there to carry me wherever I want to go? The *mestizo's* plan would take some doing. In fact, the odds of Ben winning a race seemed not even remotely possible; laughable, even. Him, win a race?

"*Mestizo,* you better come up with another idea," Ben said. His voice sounded loud in the intensely quiet desert surrounding him. Paddy nickered, thinking that Ben was talking to him.

Ben sat there a while resting, and then ran again, as far as he could, straight south. This time, he removed his hat and used his handkerchief tied around his head to absorb sweat. Now he understood why Apaches wore a cloth band around their foreheads and wore their black hair long to cover the backs of their necks from the sun. His brown hair was cropped short. This area south of town, away from water, was very desolate. Not even scrubby bushes grew here.

When he was exhausted and could not go one step further, he rolled two yellow-colored rocks together to mark the spot. He rested a while, and then ran back to Paddy. He put two more yellow rocks there also to show where it was he had started running. He folded the moccasins carefully back into the rabbit fur bag, and put his boots back on, then took a long drink from his canteen. Then he took off the handkerchief, wiped the dust off his face, and put his hat back on.

Riding back into town, he put Paddy back in the livery stable, went to his room, washed up, changed his clothing, and went to eat a big breakfast at the Horned Jackrabbit. Inside the restaurant, Brady invited Ben to sit with him at his table. During the meal, Ben made an arrangement with Brady to bring Ben's clothing to the laundry and back whenever they needed washing. The rest of that day, Ben didn't learn much that would be of help.

Around noon he went to Cavanaugh's store and bought an extra pair of black trousers, two light sand-colored shirts, and some more socks. He hated to spend the money, but he had to have clothing to wear when Brady took the dirty laundry to be done.

The next day he rose at dawn and followed the same procedure—running—carefully moving the rocks he used as markers the short extra distance he had run.

Every morning, day after day, he did the same thing, until he felt that he could run far enough, fast enough to outdistance his foe, David.

It didn't take long to realize why the Apaches wore so little clothing when they were running a long way, and he began putting aside his light brown shirt in favor of the cooler, light, sand-colored cotton shirts he bought at Cavanaugh's store.

He couldn't do anything about his broadcloth trousers; he didn't want to arouse any suspicion about what he was doing.

He left his gun, holster, and hat hanging over the saddle horn, and ran stripped down to trousers, shirt, moccasins, and headband. He was careful to avoid any area where he thought that there were miners. He didn't want anyone knowing what he was doing.

He ran with one eye out for snakes, always trying to look ahead and under shrubs. Even when he thought he was ready, he practiced an extra week, just to make sure.

The running did two things. As he ran further and further, he had time to plan out in his mind how he would try to goad David into running a race with him. That was the first thing. The second thing was completely unexpected.

He ran further than he had ever run, that last day. As he ran into the far distant southern hills and valleys surrounding Websterville on the morning that he had told himself would be the last day of practice running, he came unexpectedly on the bushwhacker. It came close to *being* his last day. And the shocking thing was, he knew the bushwhacker, slightly. Slightly.

The bushwhacker was one of the men he had inadvertently watched and gotten to know slightly by spending evenings in the Long Horn Saloon, when Ben was watching David.

Ben was running fast, and he was turning around a sharp unfamiliar bend when he came upon Adolph Ritter, kneeling in the dirt, with his carbine aimed at the back of a miner about twenty or twenty-five feet away, just over a slight rise toward the east of Ben.

Ben only had a quick look, but thought the miner was a man he had seen a few times in town named Sparky McBride, a man who had learned how to use dynamite in the War Between the States. Sparky was an older, gray-haired and gray-bearded man who was generally thought of as pleasant and with a good sense of humor. Sparky was well-liked in Websterville.

The miner—if it was Sparky—was about to be shot in the back by Ritter. Ritter, kneeling just in back of the four-foot-high mound of dirt which made up the back side of the small slope facing the miner and his mine off to the east, was taking careful aim with a new-looking carbine. The shooter was well within the range of the carbine's close deadly accuracy.

He had to do something to warn the miner!

Ben yelled, "Look out!"

Ritter turned in surprise when he heard Ben yell, and swung the rifle—a short-barreled 30-caliber that looked like U.S. Cavalry Army issue—toward Ben. It was a weapon with great fire power, and Ben was partly in shock because the barrel was so close—and aimed dead center toward his own chest now!

They were both surprised, but Ben had the momentum from running at a fast pace. He used this momentum to continue running toward Adolph Ritter and just managed to push the short barrel of the carbine to the right as Ritter fired. It was a terrible gamble, but Ben had no other choice, and he did it from instinct alone, because he had no time to think.

The rifle went off loudly as it was knocked to the side. Ritter lost his grip on the carbine, and it fell to the ground next to him. With the rifle knocked out of Ritter's hand, Ben was momentarily safe, but only until and unless he could *keep* the carbine out of the backshooter's hand.

It lay where it fell, on the ground to the right, as both men fell to the left of the rifle in a jumble of arms and legs, fighting for the upper hand.

As Ben began to wrestle Ritter, to try to keep him from reaching the shiny polished wood stock of the rifle, Ritter reached out his right hand and tried to claw his way through the dirt toward the carbine, which was lying five or six inches from Ritter's outstretched fingers. Ben cursed the fact that his own gun and rifle were back on Paddy, useless to him now.

Ben was on top of Ritter. As Ben took a swing at Ritter, he was sick at the thought of what was coming. Ritter was bigger and probably stronger than he was, and outweighed Ben by forty or fifty pounds.

Ritter was still under him, momentarily, clawing in the dirt for the rifle and Ben took advantage of that fact; he struck Ritter on the side of the chin as hard as he could and then he took one back from Ritter's left fist to the jaw that felt as if it had dislocated his jawbone. Ritter rolled back, not reaching for the carbine anymore and concentrating only on his punches.

Ritter had evidently decided that he didn't need the rifle to take care of Ben, a much smaller man. He rolled over, pushed Ben off his chest easily, and scrambled to his feet. He gave Ben another powerful punch, this time to the left temple, as Ben struggled to rise as quickly as he could and defend himself from the strong punches.

Ben saw blue, red and green stars in front of his eyes as he took another hard blow on the bone near his right eyebrow and another one on the right temple as he stood up. Ritter had punched so hard the knuckles on both of his clenched fists were bleeding.

Although Ritter was a much bigger man, Ben would not give up. He wanted to live. If Ben was going down this time; it would *not* be without a fight, he vowed to himself. He punched Ritter in the stomach as hard as he could; surprised that the big stomach was hard muscle; not soft fat.

Ritter began battering Ben by repeatedly punching him in the head, and Ben began to feel himself getting dizzy and faint. He tried to punch Ritter back in the head and face as many times as he could, but he knew he was close to getting knocked out by the repeated powerful punches to his head.

Ritter's long arms meant Ben could not keep the punches from reaching him, as hard as Ben tried to fend them off and get punches in of his own. Just as he felt himself falling, he heard a deafening noise close to his head and he thought, but wasn't sure, that his ears began ringing.

When he came to, he looked up and saw Sparky McBride standing over him, looking concerned. Sparky was holding an old battered shotgun. Ben had the feeling that he had been passed out for a few seconds—maybe even minutes.

Ben turned his head slowly and looked, and next to him, on the ground, was the dead body of Adolph Ritter, shot through the chest—dead center.

"Glad you come to. I was gettin' worried," Sparky said. "Thanks, Ben," Sparky continued gratefully. "You saved my life."

With the toe of his black leather boot, Sparky disgustedly prodded the body of the dead man lying close to Ben and continued, "Soon's he saw you was goin' down, Ritter grabbed fer the carbine and was fixin' to use it on you. Then woulda used it on me. Dangblasted bushwhacker!"

Ben sat up slowly. He saw that Sparky was right. Ritter had gone for the carbine. It was lying across his body. In fact, the barrel was touching Ben's moccasin.

"Guess I owe you, too." Ben said gratefully. "Thanks." He moved his foot so that it was no longer touching the barrel of the carbine.

"Lucky you went down when you did," Sparky said with an ironic smile. "Before that, I was aimin', but I was afraid to shoot. 'Fraid I might hit you." Sparky shook his head in bewilderment and relief. "I had no idea anyone was here, layin' fer me like that. Thought I was bein' so careful."

He spit in the dirt near the dead body of Adolph Ritter to show his disgust, then he continued. "Heard your yell. Saw Adolph turn his rifle toward you. When I saw the ruckus—what was goin' on over here, I got my shotgun and run over to see if I could help you. Lucky I had ole Betsy, here." He indicated his shotgun. "Been keepin' it close since I heard about Al

Guernsey an' the others gettin' bushwhacked. But it wouldn't have done me no good havin' ole Betsy close by if I was to get shot in the back like that bushwhacker planned."

Sparky squinted his eyes then, and looked carefully at Ben, his sense of humor showing in the expression on his face: "What in holy tarnation kind of an outfit have you got on there?"

Ben explained without going into too much detail, how he was trying to get his ranch back.

"Well, I think the way you look, all got up like an Apache with the moccasins and the sweatband around yer head, might have saved yer life." Sparky chuckled. "Ritter starin' at you in amazement an' tryin' to figger out who and what you were might have given you the couple of extry seconds that saved yer hide. Lord knows, I give you a couple of extry seconds of starin', myself, when I got over here."

Sparky grabbed Ben's hand. "Here, let me help you up." He helped Ben get to his feet. "Think you deserve a snort. Then I'll get my wagon and drag this poor excuse for a human being back to town. Tell 'em what happened. I owe you one, son. An' I won't never fer-get it. An' that there three-thousand-dollar reward the miners put up, is all yers. Heck, I paid three hunnerd dollars towards that reward myself. Money well spent, I say!"

"I'll skip the snort, and settle for a drink of water," Ben said. He thought about how far back across the desert Paddy was, and how much his own face and body hurt from the fight he had just been in. He hadn't been in a fight like that since he was a kid. His head hurt all over, front and back.

And those fights had been like practice fights, not to the death like the one he'd just been in. Truth was, his fingers were still trembling a bit, although he tried not to let Sparky see it. If Sparky noticed, he didn't let on. He just walked beside Ben companionably.

Ben had a drink of water and Sparky had his "snort" of whiskey as they stood near the small, low entrance to Sparky's mine. Then Sparky and Ben hitched up Sparky's brace of mules to his wagon and loaded the body of Adolph Ritter, non too gently, into the wagon bed.

Taking a look at the condition of Ben's face, Sparky figured out that perhaps Ben needed a ride back to Paddy. "Want a wagon ride to git yer horse?" Sparky asked.

"That'd suit me just fine," Ben said. "I've got the granddaddy of all headaches."

When they reached Paddy, Ben took off the moccasins and bandana and put on his boots and hat, and then they tied Paddy's lead onto the back of the wagon and drove to town. Ben was happy for once, not to have to ride Paddy. It was a relief to have Sparky drive the wagon. Ben had a terrible headache.

" 'Spect you know that I won't mention about your Apache fandangle runnin' outfit out there when I tell my story 'round town," Sparky said. "Far as I know, you just came upon Adolph by accident."

"That's the truth. I did come upon him by accident."

"Lucky accident fer me," Sparky said grimly.

"weren't fer you, I'd be out there roastin' in the sun, now, nothin' but buzzard meat. Course I'll have to tell the sheriff the real truth—wouldn't want to lie to him about nothin', but he's a good sort and knows when to keep his mouth shut. 'Sides, I hear he's let it be known around town that he kind of favors you. Kind of sent out the word to leave you alone."

Ben was surprised. He didn't know that. And that explained a lot about how he had been left alone and not harassed when he was doing his "detecting" in the Gold Digger's Saloon, and particularly in the Long Horn Saloon. The rough crowd there had left him alone. He had been slightly aware that he had been left alone, but he thought that it was because he was so unimportant—a nobody—to those rough men.

Now he realized that it had been due, at least partly, to Sheriff Squibb. He felt grateful to the sheriff. In a quiet way, the man was doing what he could for Ben.

Chapter Eighteen

When they reached town, a crowd gathered quickly at the wagon. Onlookers peered over into the wagon bed to see the body of Adolph Ritter.

As Ben was walking from the wagon onto the sidewalk in front of the sheriff's office, he noticed Virginia walk out of Cavanaugh's store.

He had reached the wooden sidewalk and was about ten feet away from the wagon when she approached. She was carrying a small burlap bag of Arbuckle's Coffee. She was on her way back to the restaurant, he guessed. They must have run low on coffee.

She reached Ben before she had come close enough to see what people were staring at inside the wagon. Looking at him, she said, "No! Ben, you're all bloody again! Are you all right?"

She looked stricken. He could feel his face get red in embarrassment. She must think he was a hooligan.

Seconds later, she reached the wagon and looked in. Ben saw her hear the word 'backshooter,' and enough of the story Sparky was telling, so she looked back at Ben, an apology in her eyes and in her expression. The way she looked at him gave him a funny feeling. It occurred to him again that Virginia Jackson could be quite beautiful. Especially when she looked intently at him like that, studying him as if to see that he was all right.

She paused at the wagon to hear the rest of the story Sparky was telling the crowd, and then looked at him again. Ben touched his fingers to his hat in respect and acknowledgment, and went inside Shorty Squibb's office. Shorty followed him in. Sparky stayed outside, telling the crowd about what had happened.

"Have a seat," Shorty said. "Take a load off." Shorty shut the door. Ben took the seat in front of the sheriff's desk near the window.

"What about Ritter out there in the wagon?" Ben asked.

"He ain't goin' nowhere," Shorty said wryly. "Besides, Sparky's out there with him. First, I'd like you to tell me what happened. I'll get what's left of Sparky's version later," he added wryly.

Shorty went behind his desk and sat in his oak armchair and listened without speaking as Ben began his story. Ben told the whole thing, not leaving out the part about what he was doing out there in the desert south of town.

Sheriff Squibb nodded as Ben told the story. "Judge Colby and the Woolseys aren't goin' to like hearin'

that you're a hero," Shorty said, with a smile somewhat like a grimace out of the side of his mouth.

"I'm not a hero. I got beat up."

"That ain't the way some people in town are goin'
to see it," Shorty said. "Sounds like an out-an'-out
hero story to me. Well," he continued, "best I get out
there and see to it that Ritter gets a coffin and a burial.
Need to talk to Sparky, too, if he ever stops jawin' out
there. By the way, there's a substantial reward comin'
to you for catchin' that backshooter. Three thousand
dollars."

Ben was pleased. He could use some extra money.
He remembered seeing the reward poster when he first
came back to town, and hearing Sparky speak about
it.

"I'll be in Mercer's Hotel if you need me," Ben
said. "Need to wash up and change my clothes."
Shorty nodded his head in agreement, and Ben left.
He knew people were watching him as he walked
across the street to Mercer's.

In his room, he washed, using the cold water in the
pitcher and basin to wash off the blood, and then he
changed his shirt to the light brown one. The cut near
his eyebrow was all swollen. He could feel a big lump
there, and it hurt a lot when he washed it. When he
left the hotel and walked down the street, he could
feel people looking at him.

Virginia was back in the Horned Jackrabbit when
he entered. He ordered eggs, bacon, biscuits, and coffee when she came to his table. As she stood there,

he knew from her attitude that she had heard the whole story already from Sparky.

"Sorry about the remark about your shirt. I didn't know—"

"That's all right, Miss Jackson."

"You can call me Ginny," she said. He knew she was reluctant to talk about herself, but he felt it safe to ask one question, because it was common knowledge. People had seen her arrive on the stage.

"You come in on the stage from Tucson?"

"Yes. I came out west with my Dad after the War. He died the first of January at Fort Bowie. I've been cooking and serving food ever since in Tucson, until I was invited to come up here to Websterville to work. Buckshot was an old friend of my father's."

He guessed she meant her father had been a soldier at Fort Bowie.

She added, "You better have the doctor look at that face. You have some nasty-looking lumps." Then she hurried away, as if she was embarrassed that she had stayed too long at his table, talking. When she brought his food, she placed it on the table without speaking further, and left.

He would never do anything to harm a woman, yet he had that reputation because of Lucy. He was sure that she'd heard that whole pack of lies by now. That first time, she'd stood so close. . . . He only hoped that what Lucy had done hadn't soured Ginny on him.

She'd acted, though, as if she was real worried about him when she saw that he was bloody again. He could only hope . . . No wonder she was cautious. He was probably the last man in town any woman wanted to have anything to do with. He was surprised she was as nice to him as she was.

He heard Buckskin tell her, "Tomorrow's your day off." He ate and then left, and went back to his hotel room. He was going to wait no longer. Tonight was the night that he would set his plan in motion.

He wasn't in his room five minutes when he heard a knock on the door. Expecting Brady, he said, "Who is it?"

He heard a muffled answer. It sounded to him like the voice—spoken softly as if the person didn't want anyone else in the hotel to hear—said the name Woolsey. Dang! He'd had enough excitement for one day. And his bruised face hurt in three or four places besides his eyebrow.

"Just a minute," he said. He strapped on his gun, and made sure that it was tied down, and that the Navy Colt was loose in the holster. Then he slowly opened the door.

John Woolsey stood there, his hat in his hands. He had no gunbelt on. He was neatly dressed in a new-looking black broadcloth suit with a white shirt. He had on a black silk neatly tied tie. A black matching vest, inside his suit jacket, had a lot of small black buttons. He wore shiny, new-looking boots. He looked very prosperous: the perfect banker. His yellow hair, which was beginning to have a few gray hairs here and there, like his mustache, was also clipped short and looked neat.

Nervously he said, "May I come in?"

Grudgingly, Ben let him in.

John came inside the small room and pretended to look around. He turned his hat around by the brim, as if trying to think of what to say. Finally, he managed, "Heard about what you did this morning. That was a fine thing you did, saving Sparky." Then he was silent.

Ben was in no mood for small talk. He wanted John Woolsey to say what he had to say and get out. After what John Woolsey had done to him, and what he had threatened Jim Magee with at the livery stable, he was lucky that Ben didn't punch him—or worse.

The thought of punching anyone suddenly struck Ben as funny. His face and body were already beat up enough for one day, in fact, enough for a lot of days. Not to mention the area on his back that was still tender from his recent bullet wound. He was, in fact, pretty much of a mess.

"What is it that you want, John?" Ben said, stiffly.

"Nothing. I—" John Woolsey glanced around. It seemed to hit him that Ben lived in the hotel now, instead of out at the ranch. His face looked pained, as he looked around and saw the few things Ben still owned.

There wasn't much. Two large canvas bags, the rabbit fur bag, a few items of clothing, and the Remington in its leather sheath hung over the closest bedpost near the pillow at the head of the bed. He looked at Ben.

"May I sit down a minute?"

Ben nodded a silent, reluctant agreement, and John Woolsey sat on the edge of the bed farthest away from the gunbelt, near the foot of the small single bed. Ben guessed that John really had nothing much to say. He was here to find out as much as he could about Ben's plans.

"Ben," John said hesitantly, "you can do me a lot of harm." What John said, and the almost whining way that he said it, only irritated Ben; it did not win Ben's sympathy. How did the man sitting there have the *nerve* to sit there and say that, after what he had done to Ben? Ben walked back in forth in front of the bed, debating whether to throw this man out of his room.

What can I say back to give this man even an inkling of the harm he has already done to me? Is there any way to impress on this man what he has done? Ben knew from the way John sat there, that John was only capable of thinking selfishly, about himself and his own problems.

He really didn't care about what he had done to Ben. John only wanted to make his own life easier, smoother. Ben felt only disgust for this man, much older than he was—almost his own father's age. A man who should have known better than to do what he had done to Ben: pretended he had witnessed a bill of sale that never happened! Put his signature on forged paperwork!

"Why did you lie and say that you were a witness to my selling the ranch to Ollie?" Ben said, harshly, without a trace of sympathy in his voice.

"Lucy—"

"Lucy?"

"Lucy said that after Ollie's death, you went into

her bedroom and destroyed the papers that showed that you had sold your part of the ranch to Ollie."

"And you believed her?"

"Why wouldn't I? She was going to be coming into my family. She was going to be a family member . . . marry my son. Why wouldn't I believe her?"

Ben walked over and stood looking out the window into the street, but he wasn't really seeing what was down there. He was concentrating on listening to what John was saying. When John was finished, there was silence in the room. Finally Ben spoke. "She lied. She lied to you. *Because I never sold my half of the ranch to anyone!* I wanted to leave because I didn't like Lucy. But Ollie asked me to stay," Ben said fiercely and bitterly, picturing Ollie in his mind.

"Whose idea was it to forge my signature on the fake papers, John?" Ben said harshly.

"Why, Lucy's, of course. She said that that was the only way that justice could be done, after what you had done. You had burned the papers which showed that you had sold your half of the ranch to Ollie—"

"Did it ever occur to you to come and *ask* me?" Ben said. "Give me a chance to tell the truth?"

"Lucy said that you would just lie. Maybe even do away with her. So we thought it best—"

"—To lie and commit forgery. Not to mention steal my half of the ranch?"

"Honestly, we didn't think of it that way. We thought we were just helping Lucy get what was rightfully hers. And to tell you the truth, David was so in love with her—" John put his head down into his hands. It was the first faint sign of honest remorse that Ben had seen out of the man.

"I didn't even tell my wife what we had done. I knew she would try to talk me out of it. Only David, Lucy, and myself knew what we had done. Later, I began to suspect—"

"What? That Lucy was a liar?" Ben couldn't keep the disgust out of his voice.

"Then when everyone in town ganged up on us the night that you rode out of town, I began to realize that perhaps Lucy had pulled the wool over my—our—eyes, mine *and* David's. You looked at me with such hate that day—But he was so in love with her—."

Lucy had that effect on men, Ben had to grant that.

"And after you rode off, Lucy's said and done things that made me realize that she's . . . well, a liar. She hasn't been a wife to David. She threw him off the . . . your ranch on Cedar Creek. She's done some things. . . . I caught her in lies, and I think, so has David."

Ben thought of what Mrs. Mercer had said about John Woolsey not being able to sleep nights. Still, Ben was not sorry for the expensively dressed man sitting on his bed, trying to get his sympathy. And John was not being completely honest.

Ben was careful not to mention what he knew about John Woolsey's visit to Jimmy Magee's livery stable to find out what he could about Ben. Jimmy had mentioned that in confidence.

"What are you going to do?" John asked. Clearly, John Woolsey was worried. Worried even more now that Sparky McBride was going about town proclaiming Ben a hero to anyone who'd listen.

"I don't know," Ben said, honestly. What was there to do? Judge Colby had already indicated that he wouldn't change his judgement on the matter. "Are you willing to go to the judge and tell him the truth?" Ben said.

"No. I couldn't do that," John Woolsey said, his lower lip trembling. "I have to think of what that would do to my wife and my son David. I'd be disgraced . . . and the bank. . . . I just can't do that. I'll never publicly admit what I've done."

Ben walked over to the door and opened it.

"I guess then, our talk is over."

John Woolsey stood up and walked to the door.

"I'm sorry, Ben."

"So am I." Ben said curtly and stiffly, and he closed the door behind Woolsey harder than he meant to. In fact, it slammed shut.

"Coward," Ben muttered at the absent John, disgusted, as he walked over to his bed and sat and put his hands on his hurting head.

John Woolsey had admitted his part in it privately to Ben, but what good would that do if he wouldn't admit it publicly?

What did John Woolsey want? Forgiveness? Forgiveness without accepting any of the consequences of his wrongdoing? Or had he come here to find out, as best he could, what Ben was going to do next? That was the option that made the most sense, knowing John Woolsey as he now did. He no longer thought that John Woolsey was a good, honest man. He was a coward. And he would probably never change. His visit to Ben was self-serving, and Ben would never trust him again.

Chapter Nineteen

Ben pushed open the doors of the Long Horn Saloon and went in. Because of John Woolsey's visit, he was a little late arriving. David Woolsey was inside. It was after nine o'clock at night, and the "regulars" were all there, already drinking. Some had been there since early afternoon.

And tonight was different because as Ben walked inside, all heads turned and looked at him. He was no longer the "invisible" man, the non-person. Everyone inside had heard the story that Sparky McBride had been telling all day long.

In fact, Sparky came over as soon as Ben entered and walked Ben to the table over to the left where he had been sitting. One of the six men actually left the table and came back with a chair for Ben to sit on. This was genteel treatment from a group of men who were usually rough and rowdy and prided themselves on it.

David was directly across the table from Ben.

This was the perfect night—the perfect opportunity—but how to go about it, getting the conversation around to where he wanted it to go?

How?

Ben couldn't think of anything; despite how long he had planned for such an opportunity. Here he was, sitting at a table with David, and he had no idea how to begin. He wanted to challenge David to a race. A race for the ownership of the ranch. But how to go about it?

He was stumped.

Worse, everyone was being very nice and courteous and respectful to him. A couple of the men at the table were miners and they were happy that there was one less bushwhacker—claim jumper—to worry about. They all wanted to buy Ben drinks. But drinks was not what Ben was here for.

This hardly seemed to be the night and the place to challenge anyone to a race. He was being treated like an honored guest—like a king. He could sense that David didn't like that.

Ben waited, and as the night wore on, he was accepted as one of the group. It was with cautious respect at first, but he was treated more normally after the group had had a few more drinks. Finally, the men's attention strayed and they forgot about Ben and began to taunt each other about physical prowess.

Soon, David and a man named Cyrus Dubbs began arm wrestling.

It wasn't long before David had beaten Cyrus Dubbs. Dubbs left in a foul humor shortly after, and David couldn't resist, the pompous fool! He looked Ben directly in the eyes. "Hey, Mr. Bruised Face, how about arm wrestling me, since you're such a big hero these days?" David asked with a smirk that said that he was sure of winning. He wanted to take Ben down a peg in everyone's eyes.

"I'm not much at arm wrestling," Ben said slowly and carefully. "That's a sport for youngsters, isn't it?" There, the bait was out. He'd done it.

David's face, usually red, reddened even more. He was the local champion of sorts of the Long Horn arm wrestlers, and to be told that it was a sport only for children had got his attention—and his dander up.

"Youngsters? Youngsters, you say?" David said angrily, insulted.

Ben deliberately played it slow and easy, as if he were the most relaxed man in the place. In fact, he was very tense inside. He only hoped it didn't show. He picked up his whiskey and took a tantalizingly slow, small sip. David was glaring at him now, his eyes narrowed into slits. In a pleasant voice, as if it were the most unimportant thing he could say, Ben said slowly, "No offense."

Oh, Lord, how can I put this? I've got to say this exactly right! Casually he said, putting his glass down on the table as slowly as he could, "Now, as I see it, a strong arm is all right. But that's only a small part of a man's body." He deliberately paused, as if thinking. "It seems to me you need a contest that takes into account the man's whole body, if a man *really* wants to prove that he's the *best.*"

There! Ben had thrown the baited hook into the water. David was a man who always wanted—*had*—to be the best. Would David take the bait?

"What do you mean?" David said, angrily glaring at Ben. David leaned forward toward Ben and got up off his seat an inch or two in a threatening manner, closing his right hand into a fist. Ben knew that David wanted to come around the table and punch him. He was that angry.

"Just what do you mean by that?" David said.

Ben forced himself to smile as if the whole argument meant nothing to him. "I didn't mean anything by it. . . . I only meant that—" here he pretended to be thinking again, making David and the others wait in suspense. "I meant that a contest that took into account the whole man . . . the whole body . . . would be better than *puny* arm wrestling."

Two of the other men at the table, Fred Schlagel and Gilbert Muldoon, seemed to be thinking over what Ben had said, and they both nodded their heads in agreement. Cyrus Dubbs, who had walked over to the bar, walked back to the table and stood behind Fred Schlagel, listening. David had a perplexed look on his face, but he seemed to be thinking it over.

"What, then? How about a horse race?" Fred Schlagel said.

"No, stupid," Gilbert Muldoon said. "That just

shows how fast yer horse is. We need something that shows how good yer whole self is—yer body. That's the test of a man's strength. Yer whole body."

With a grin and a conspiring smirk at Ben that showed that Sparky knew exactly what Ben was leading up to, Sparky said, as if he had just thought about it, "A foot race. That's what would measure who was the *best*. Yep. That's what we need. A foot race. A test of the strength of the whole man."

David looked around the table. A big grin spread over his face as he sized up all the men at the table. Ben could see that David was thinking that he was superior to all these men. David looked as if he wanted to laugh out loud. Most of these men had been drinking all afternoon. He could beat any one of them in a race, with his hands tied behind his back.

"All right." David said, gleefully. "Which one of you drunken galoots will take me on in a foot race?"

No one answered. Even Cyrus Dubbs was silent.

"I will." Ben said quietly.

There was dead silence as it sunk in around the table. No one raised their glass as Ben continued, "Tomorrow. Eight o'clock in the morning. You put up the ranch that Lucy took from me, and I'll put up my reward money."

They all seemed to have heard about the reward money, or seen the posters around town. As that sunk in, Ben added, "And let's make this race interesting. We'll race from the foothills of Anderson Mountain back to Sheriff Squibb's office. First one who reaches Sheriff Squibb's door is the winner."

There was an intake of breath as the full impact of the distance sunk in.

Gilbert Muldoon said in a shocked voice, "Why, that's a mighty long way."

Ben smiled. "What about it, David? Are you willing to bet you're the best?"

All the men knew that as Lucy's husband, David had the power to sign over any property they owned. David looked a little uncertain, but he didn't want to back out in front of all his friends. He was trapped by his own ego. "I'm in," David said.

"Tomorrow, then," Sparky said. "As agreed. From the foot of Anderson Mountain back to town. Eight o'clock tomorrow morning. First man to reach the sheriff's office wins. If David wins, he gets Mitchell's reward money. Ben wins, he gets Cedar Creek Ranch back. Agreed?"

"Agreed." Ben said, exulting inside, but casual on the outside.

"Agreed." David said. But he didn't look happy about it.

Chapter Twenty

Ben lay in his bed in the hot hotel room, unable to sleep. He kept thinking about Miguel. He wanted to get the ranch back as much for Miguel's sake as his own.

Ben knew Miguel had had a lot of trouble in his life that was not his fault. Miguel had been born in a small town in northern Mexico. When he was just a baby, a crazy lady some people in the village thought had "special powers" had seen Miguel outside his house one day, playing in the dirt. After taking a look at Miguel, she told everyone in the village that Miguel was special. That Miguel would grow up to have "special—magical—powers". People in the village believed her.

Somehow, renegade Apaches in the area heard the story and came early one morning and murdered all the villagers and stole the boy. They wanted the boy with "special powers." They thought that he could protect them from both Mexican and and U.S. Army soldiers.

Unfortunately, the Apaches found out shortly that Miguel was just a normal boy. Luckily, an Apache woman took Miguel in anyway. Miguel ran away to Texas as soon as he could, and ended up on Ben's parents' ranch. He had lived all of his adult life as a part of the Mitchell family—until Lucy came along.

The crazy old woman who said that Miguel had special powers had caused a lot of damage to a lot of people. She had caused a lot of villagers to be killed, including herself. Although Ben had heard the story—now almost a legend—of Miguel's childhood ever since he was a child, Miguel himself had never talked about it.

Ben tossed and turned in the bedclothes, scolding himself for thinking about all this when he should be sleeping. Finally, late, he fell asleep. He had a headache when he woke up.

There was a surprisingly large group of people already there as Ben walked out of Mercer's Hotel at seven o'clock the next morning. The group already had their horses saddled and ready to ride. Most had canteens hanging from their saddles. Ben smiled as he saw that Sparky had one of his own mules saddled as well as Ben's horse Paddy saddled and ready to go. Sparky was standing near the hitching post in front of Mercer's Hotel with the two animals. He saw that Sparky had a canteen hanging from Paddy's saddle.

David rode up on a large brown gelding. He was

not in the best of moods and curtly nodded to Sparky and Ben. He patted his pocket to show that he had the deed to the Cedar Creek Ranch in his possession. David had on black trousers and a loose, white cotton shirt.

Ben patted his pocket to show that he had signed a paper which turned the money from the reward over to David if Ben lost the race. He had written it out last night in the hotel room. David acknowledged that he saw.

Then Ben noticed a few feet behind David, riding sidesaddle on one of the horses Ben had bred and trained at Cedar Creek ranch—as angry as he'd ever seen anyone in his life—was Lucy. Her eyes were shooting fire, practically, she was so furious. She narrowed her eyes and gave Ben the most intensely angry look he'd ever seen. Ben was sure that she and David had had a huge argument, either last night or this morning. If she had had a gun at this moment, she'd have been very dangerous.

John Woolsey was nowhere to be seen. Neither was the Judge. Sheriff Squibb came out of his office and looked at Lucy. Lucy ignored everyone, glaring at Ben and David, alternately. Somehow, David had managed to get the deed from her. David was keeping his word. Ben was really happy about that.

The group had grown to about forty people as they rode southwest from town to the foothills of Anderson Mountain. As the group stopped, Ben and David dismounted. Brady came over and took Paddy, and James Magee took the reins of David's horse. Both men walked to the front of the group of people and faced back toward town.

Ben took off his hat and handed it to Sparky, took his blue bandana out of his pocket and tied it around his head as a sweat band. He looked over and was surprised to see that David took off his own hat, handed it to Sparky, untied his red bandana from around his neck and copied what Ben had done.

Ben looked down. Ben had on his moccasins, and David had on a pair of well-worn regular black leather shoes. The shoes looked comfortable and well broken in, as if they had had a lot of wear.

Sheriff Squibb spoke first, and with authority. "Everyone is to stay at least thirty feet to each side of the runners. Anyone edging any closer," Here he pointedly looked at Lucy, "will have to answer to me."

Mrs. Mercer was driving a wagon with Ginny Jackson as a passenger, and Doctor and Mrs. Burns were in another wagon. Most of the other spectators were on horseback.

"I'll be taking the papers, now, and I'll be holding them until the race is decided," Sheriff Squibb said. Ben handed over the reward money voucher and David handed over the deed. The sheriff folded the two papers together and put them in his pocket.

"Winner takes all," the sheriff announced, then he took out his Colt .45 and pointed it into the air. James Magee took a stick and drew a line in the dirt in front of the place the two men stood. People on horseback who knew that their horses would be startled at the sound of close gunfire backed away a safe distance.

Ben looked sideways at his opponent. Stripped to his shirt, trousers, shoes, and bandana, and without the black broadcloth jacket that David usually wore as a businessman, Ben was surprised to see that David was leaner and more muscled than he had previously thought. Doc Burns came over and placed their canteen of water around each man's neck on a leather strap. When Ben pushed the canteen around to the back of him, David looked over and did the same.

David looked over and grinned down at Ben. He, too, was comparing their physical conditions. "I already won this," David said confidently, looking at the difference in size between the two of them. "Look at you. You're pint size. I'm a quart size. You're nothing but a peanut."

Ben knew what David was doing. He was trying to discourage Ben before the race even started. He looked around for Ginny. She was looking at him, and she smiled encouragement. She didn't seem at all worried.

He turned back and faced the direction toward town. *Mestizo, I hope you were right.* Ben looked down at the moccasins. *I'm counting on the gift you gave me. And not just the gift of the moccasins; the gift of your wisdom. I just hope you were right: "In the short race, the big man wins. In the longer race, the short man wins."*

The gun went off, and Ben was a second behind already because he had been thinking about the *mestizo* as the shot rang out. Dang! He began running.

He could hear some voices cheering him, and some cheering David as he set off, running as hard as he could. A few minutes into the race, David was draw-ing ahead. David kept the lead that he had at the be-ginning.

At times, Ben looked and it seemed that David was drawing ahead even further. He looked over, and to the side, sure enough, looking at him, gloating that he was behind, was Lucy. She had set the pace of her horse to keep up with *him*, mocking *him*. Not David. He was aware that Sheriff Squibb was riding nearby, keeping an eye on Lucy for him. He forced himself to try and put her mocking presence out of his mind and concentrate on what he was doing. But she was a dis-traction. And dang! It was already hot.

As he ran, he cursed himself over and over for being such a fool—thinking that he could win this race. And worse, he had gambled with the reward money he could have used to bring Miguel back from Texas. It was partially the thought of getting Miguel back that helped him not to give up as David disappeared into the distance, now probably over a mile ahead—at least. He ran, thinking of Miguel.

As Ben ran, he thought about how wonderful it would be if he had the ranch back. Miguel could live out the rest of his life in peace, knowing he would always have a home. Ben ran on, looking for a glimpse—any sign—that he was catching up to David. He wasn't.

Once, in the far distance in front of him, he saw a large puff of dust rise up, and he guessed that David had fallen. Some other larger clouds of dust he knew to be riders who were keeping up with David, off to the side. He hoped enough people stayed up there who were Ben's friends to be sure that no one cheated and gave David a ride up on a horse.

But that puff Ben saw directly ahead of him—had David already fallen once? This gave him a bit of hope and spurred him on. It also made him realize that he'd better pay attention to what he was doing so that he didn't take a big tumble, himself. He had to watch out for rocks in his path.

He had been running for quite a while now, and he was getting tired. In the distance, he saw the tiny skinny white point that he knew was the church steeple where Lucy had married Ollie—and David.

Off to the side of him, he saw groups of people who were keeping up with him instead of David. He saw that Ginny was there, on horseback. She smiled once as he glanced over. She didn't seem at all worried. In fact, she made a small circle with her thumb and the finger next to it that meant that he had it made; he was going to win. She kneed her horse and rode on ahead; well off to the left side, out of his path.

He kept running. He grabbed the leather strap and pulled the canteen around to the front of him, pulled off the stopper and took a few swigs. Immediately, he felt better. He put the stopper back in as best he could and kept on running, swinging the leather strap under his arm again until the canteen was again at his back.

Suddenly, he saw ahead of him, small in the distance, a glimpse of David's white shirt. He was catching up! And he guessed that they both had about half the distance yet to go.

Was David slowing down? Yes, he was! *Yea for you, mestizo!*

David's back grew larger as the seven or so miles left grew to six, and then five. The town of Websterville was out there in the distance.

Ben took some more drinks out of the canteen. He saw David do the same. Gradually, the small buildings and steeple grew larger and larger. And finally, Ben was catching up, and then, yes, passing David! David's usually red face was even more bright red. He was breathing hard and having trouble catching his breath. But Ben knew enough not to take anything for granted.

Still, he felt himself pull slowly ahead, and although he didn't turn to look to see where David was, by the lack of the sound of running feet close behind him and the lack of the sound of another person breathing and clothing rustling, he knew that he was pulling further and further ahead!

As he came to the edge of town, he was thrilled and happy to see his group of friends—people that he knew in town including Jimmy Magee, Doc and Mrs. Burns, Jeb Skeggs, Mrs. Mercer, and others dismounted and waiting for him to run up the last part of the street.

He ran past the church and on up toward the sheriff's office, where he could see Ginny waiting for him near the front of the crowd. She had dismounted and was standing near the door. Her eyes were shining, and she looked as if she was crying. Was she crying with happiness? For him?

As he reached Sheriff Squibb's door, he slowed down, reached out, and touched it. He was very tired and had a hard time catching his own breath. His chest was heaving up and down, and he was breathing hard, but he was a happy man.

Ginny came over quietly and gave him a hug.

"I'm all sweaty," he said.

"I don't care," she said. "I'm very happy for you." And Ben hugged her back.

Sheriff Squibb handed Ben the deed to Cedar Creek ranch and the voucher for the reward money. "Congratulations. You are the owner again of Cedar Creek Ranch!" The Sheriff seemed very pleased. "I'll need to talk to you a little later," Sheriff Squibb said. "I have something important to tell you." He smiled at Ben and Ginny.

"I'll be in your office in a couple of minutes," Ben said. Somehow, he found himself gently holding Ginny's hand.

In a moment, between all the congratulations he was receiving, he asked Ginny if she would like to take a ride out and see the ranch after he washed up and changed his clothes. She answered, "Yes" breathlessly, her eyes sparkling. There was something there—between the two of them—and he thought she felt it too, by the way she looked back at him, as he quietly held her hand in his. If things worked out he would make sure that for the rest of her life she would not have to work so hard as she had since her father died.

People were coming up and pounding Ben on the back, congratulating him. All he could think of, beside

Ginny, who was standing close to him, was that now he could send for Miguel.

It was over an hour before he got a chance to return to Shorty Squibb's office. He'd needed to return to the hotel to wash and pack up, and pay his bill. He arranged to meet Ginny in a half hour.

Brady brought hot water to his hotel room for Ben to wash the dirt and dust off. When Ben got back home to the ranch, one of the first things he wanted to do, was to soak in a long hot bath—right after he showed Ginny around.

When he walked back out onto the street a short while later, the first thing he saw and heard was a big public argument going on between Lucy and David, which culminated with Lucy storming off. He heard her yell "California!" and get into a packed-up wagon. It was driven by a man Ben had never seen.

Sparky McBride, the miner, who was standing close to Lucy as she and David were arguing, came over as Lucy stormed off, climbed into the loaded-up wagon, and drove off. Sparky was chuckling. "Seems Lucy is all packed up and leaving for California."

"Poor California," Ben said. Ginny was nowhere to be seen yet, so he went to the livery stable next, where he loaded Paddy up, and paid James Magee. Then he went to send a telegram to the Barnes ranch in Texas to tell Miguel to return to Websterville. The message said: "Money on the way shortly. Lucy gone for good. Come home. Ben." He had one more thing to do, and then he was going home. Home.

He walked over to the sheriff's office and went inside. Shorty was sitting behind his desk with a pleased smile on his face. "So, you're having a good day, I guess. I need to tell you a couple of things." Shorty said, leaning back in the chair behind his desk. Shorty was referring to Ginny as well as the race, Ben knew.

Ben grinned. He could see that Shorty was pleased about something besides Ben winning the race and Ginny. "You look like the cat that caught the canary, sheriff," Ben said.

"I did catch me a big female canary, so to speak," Shorty said. "I did me some checking—which I am the first to admit, I should have done a long time ago. I'm not too proud to admit that. But anyway, here it is. I called in some favors from a friend of mine down in Tucson, and he did some checking around for me. Seems Lucy has been married at least once before. Husband number one is still alive and in Tucson. So she, in effect, was never really legally married to either your brother *or* David Woolsey. She was never entitled to the ranch.

"Second. Another very interesting fact. It somewhat accounts for how strange Judge Colby has been acting since Lucy arrived. Seems Lucy's name—her maiden name—was Colby. She's the judge's niece. Seems she knows a few secrets about the judge that he would prefer to keep secret. My, oh, my, does that fact explain a few things? I'll need to be speaking to both of them shortly."

"Well, you'd better hurry, then, because gossip is, Lucy's leaving for California," Ben said. "Man I don't know drove off in a wagon with her."

"I don't think she'll be leaving for anywhere, except the hoosegow for fraud, at the very least. And her uncle might very well accompany her."

"Prison?"

"Yep. And I'll be interested to find out who the man with her in the wagon is. If it is her real husband, that might prove interesting. If it is some new unsuspecting poor sucker, well—And I want to talk to the Judge about his connection to the claim jumpers and Adolph Ritter." Ben stood up to leave, and the sheriff added, "Two more things. The reward money from the Miner's Association. It will be here in a couple of days. I'll stop out at the ranch with it as soon as it arrives."

"Thanks."

"And I got a return telegram about Sam Logan— the Lost Prospector's family. All deceased. Some sort of range war going on down there, as well as some sickness in the family since ol' Sam left. Nobody left to claim the nuggets; so I guess they're yours." The Sheriff reached into a drawer of his desk, and pulled out the small sack that Ben had found. He handed it to Ben.

"I'd like to keep the holster and gun myself, if you don't mind," the sheriff said, "as keepsakes. Ol' Sam Logan was a friend of mine."

"Not at all," Ben said, tucking the small pouch into his shirt pocket. A minute later Ben left the sheriff's office, and saw Ginny hurry joyfully toward him, her eyes shining with happiness for him. It was going to be fun getting to know her better.

Today, he felt he was the luckiest man in the world! His ranch back, Ginny at his side, and Miguel soon to be on his way home! *All right, mestizo,* he thought, *maybe not the luckiest, but certainly the most fortunate!*